ASHAMED

Steven Lundle

Copyright © 2021 Steven Lundle

All rights reserved

The characters and events portrayed in this book are fictitious. Any similarity to real persons, living or dead, is coincidental and not intended by the author.

No part of this book may be reproduced, or stored in a retrieval system, or transmitted in any form or by any means, electronic, mechanical, photocopying, recording, or otherwise, without express written permission of the publisher.

ISBN-13: 9798512025703

Cover design by: Hedri

I dedicate this to everyone out there who has ever felt ashamed for being who they are. Remember that you are loved. Regardless of how others make you feel, your feelings and identity are valid. Things will get better.

CONTENTS

Title Page
Copyright
Dedication
Introduction
Chapter 1 — 1
Chapter 2 — 15
Chapter 3 — 26
Chapter 4 — 38
Chapter 5 — 52
Chapter 6 — 63
Acknowledgement — 71
About The Author — 73
Books By This Author — 75

INTRODUCTION

Although this book is a work of fiction, almost everything that occurs was based on some event in my life. I was raised in rural Alberta, Canada in a strict fundamentalist environment. In the 90s and early 2000s, I attended the Mayerthorpe Christian Academy, which was a fundamentalist Christian School located in the basement of a Baptist Church in the small town of Mayerthorpe. It was very strict there. They used corporal punishment, which I was subjected to once. I was probably about ten or eleven at the time, but those memories have stayed with me up into adulthood. I also recall a girl getting in trouble for having a skirt that only went to her knees. Those of us who were into the Pokemon craze at that time were told that Pokemon was evil and that they were named after literal demons.

During my time there, I developed crushes on a couple of the other boys, but I knew that was something I absolutely couldn't allow anyone to know about. Canada was talking about legalizing same sex marriage and the subject was very controversial in our community.

The curriculum we used was from Texas and was very outdated. They taught absurd things: That socialized medicine was evil, that women had to be submissive to their husbands, and that a girl showing the slightest amount of skin above the ankles would cause men to have impure thoughts.

I was about twelve or thirteen by the time the school closed down, but my mom refused to let us go to the public school. We were homeschooled with the same curriculum.

I was twenty when I moved to Edmonton. I found myself messed up, both emotionally and academically, and I was not fully prepared for adult life in a secular world. I learned quickly, and I was so lucky to meet so many supportive and loving people. It was through meeting people in the gay community that I became comfortable with my own sexuality, and I learned to accept myself for who I am.

I have since moved on and am currently living my best life doing what I love, which includes travelling and teaching, as well as writing and working on independent films. Where possible, I try to bring attention to LGBTQ issues, and i hope that no other kid has to feel that they need to suppress their sexuality like I did.

If you want to get in touch and keep up to date with my writing and film work, you can find me on Facebook.

www.facebook.com/Steven-Lundle-100499765485457
Also, check out my Production Company on Facebook. All my short films are available on Youtube.

www.facebook.com/KoyamaProductionsInc
www.youtube.com/user/koyamacorp

CHAPTER 1

This happened many years ago, yet I still remember that day as if it just happened. The memories of that public act of humiliation have haunted me until adulthood.

Usually, my mother drove me to school, but on this particular day, it was my father. He worked the night shift at a local factory and was going to take me to school after coming home. Other than that, the day started as usual. I got myself up at 6:00 AM, took a hot shower, and then poured myself a heaping bowl of cereal before taking a seat on the sofa. I stared out at our snow-covered garden and shivered as I took my first bite. Winter was my least favorite season. At 6:30, it was still dark outside. It made me feel sad looking out at the black nothingness that was our front yard. I promised myself that as soon as I turned eighteen; I'd move somewhere that never saw snow.

There was two feet of snow and a sidewalk that wouldn't shovel itself. I'd be forced to do it at some point, but I figured I could put it off until the afternoon, given what was about to happen. Considering what was going to happen, that was the least of my worries.

As I sat there, deep in thought, I heard shuffling feet behind me. My siblings were getting up and getting ready. Usually, I helped them, but on this day, I wasn't in the mood. I had too much going on.

I was the oldest of six children, and my mother was expecting number seven. My mother worked full time as a nurse at our local hospital, and my father slept during the day, so I took on a lot of responsibility taking care of my younger brothers and sisters. I usually had no problem doing that. But today just wasn't the day for me.

I heard the clunk of a bowl on the kitchen counter, followed by the sound of cereal spilling all over the floor. I rolled my eyes and downed the last of my milk. They were old enough that they could clean up their own mess.

I returned my attention to the outside. I could make out the snowflakes falling softly to the ground from our outside porch light. I had to admit that it was a pretty sight, despite my disdain for winter. My problem wasn't really the snow, but the cold that came with it. Headlights caught my attention and indicated the approach of my father's old Chevy truck as he pulled up into our driveway.

I slid off the sofa and dropped my dishes into the kitchen sink before making my way to my bedroom. I stayed in there longer than I needed to. My father would definitely talk to me about today, and I wanted to hold that off for as long as possible.

I brushed my teeth for a little longer than was necessary and washed my face before putting on my uniform. We attended a Christian School that was strict about attire, and they required us to wear uniforms.

When I heard a soft knock on the door, I was putting on my tie while I looked at myself in my full-length mirror. At fourteen years old, I was tall for my age. I was skinny with short-cropped hair. My school banned boy's hair that touched the ears, so they forced me to keep mine short. My uniform consisted of navy blue pants, a white dress shirt, and a blue tie. The tie was always the part that I hated the most. It was such a pain to get it perfectly straight. I swore to myself that after graduating, I would never wear a tie again.

My dad knocked once more before sticking his head in my room. His face was stern and serious, but his voice was gentle enough. "Hey Jeremiah, are you ready to go?"

I glanced at him before looking back at my reflection. I was getting frustrated. I just couldn't get this stupid tie to sit straight.

"Here, let me help you with that," my dad said as he stepped in and got on his knees to be at my eye level. At over six feet, he was pretty tall. That's where I got it from, as my mom was on the short side.

With my tie finally on proper, it was time to go. I took my time putting on my winter jacket and then grabbed my backpack. I followed my dad out to the truck. He left running to keep it warm. I slid in beside him, and we pulled out of the driveway. It was getting light now. We lived on an acreage, and it was a thirty-minute drive into town, which is why we were leaving so early.

"Aren't the others coming with?" I asked.

"Your mother will bring them a little later. I wanted to have some alone time with you."

"Oh," was all I could mutter. This would be a horrible day. I knew it.

We drove about ten minutes along the gravel road before we reached the highway. There was a wind, and the road was quite sleek, so we drove below the speed limit. It was going to take longer than usual. I could feel the minutes dragging by.

About fifteen minutes without anyone saying anything, my dad reached for the truck radio and turned it off. It played a sermon by a well-known TV evangelist. My dad went right into the events of the day. "You know why this has to happen, don't you?"

I didn't like the tone in his voice, but I knew better than to say something about it, so I said a simple, "Yea." I didn't understand why they had to make such a public issue about this in all honesty. But I knew enough to answer in a way that was expected. Just shut up and agree. That was my life.

There was another moment of silence before my dad spoke again. "Your mom and I are very disappointed in you. You should know better. Is this how we raised you? To be dishonest?"

"No," I mumbled. I glanced at the truck's analog clock. I just wanted to be there already.

"This isn't finished after school. Your mom and I need to have a talk about this tonight as well."

"What? Why? Isn't the punishment at school enough?"

"I guess that depends on how much your attitude changes. Be gracious about this, and we will take that into consideration when deciding your punishment."

I was red in the face by this point. It wasn't fair. What I did wasn't even that bad. Not bad enough to warrant all of this. I knew better to argue, but I could feel the anger welling up inside of me.

"If someone could have helped me like I asked, then this wouldn't have happened," I said.

"That still doesn't give you any excuse," my dad said. His voice was stern, and I knew better than to keep arguing. I clenched my fist, punched myself hard on the side of my leg, and held my hand there for a moment. I was fuming inside, and it took all I had to keep my temper in check.

When we arrived at the school, I couldn't get out fast enough. Our school met in the basement of a Baptist Church. It was the most conservative one in our entire town. I ran up the steps of the church without looking back at my dad.

In the foyer, I met Mr. Johnson, the school principal. He was a friendly but strict man who had his own view of what the Bible said, and he left no room for other interpretations. He was regarded in our community as a man of authority, and he managed the school with an iron fist.

Mr. Johnson greeted me with a smile, and he gave my father a warm handshake. They exchanged pleasantries before turning their attention back to me.

"You can go put your things on your desk, and then Ms. Anderson will lead you up to the sanctuary," Mr. Johnson said.

Under normal circumstances, I didn't mind his thick Tennessee accent, but now it irritated me. I nodded as I hung my jacket on the hangar. I placed my winter boots on the mat and went downstairs.

The large fellowship room was converted during the week into the *"Learning Center"*. That was to say, our classroom. There were about 30 students, all from grades 1 - 12. We worked independently in our own cubicles. They looked like desks at a telemarketing company. If we needed help, we raised a miniature replica of the American flag, and a class monitor would come to see what we needed help with. Otherwise, we were on our own, and we worked independently. We used study packs and didn't receive any outside instruction.

It was early, and students were still arriving. I made my way to my desk and took out my study packs, organizing them on my desk. As I did so, he caught my eye. His name was Ricky. He was the only non-white student at our school. His family had just moved to our small town of 2,000 people. They had immigrated from the Philippines, and Ricky started studying here at the beginning of the school year.

They attended our church on Sundays as well. He had two older sisters who already graduated and worked with their mom in her food catering business. Ricky and I became fast friends. But there was something else as well. I couldn't explain it, but I really enjoyed his company. More than with my other church friends. I don't know how to explain it, but there was something different about him. He seemed to understand me better than most other people. We had a connection.

I could only hang out with kids from the church. Other kids in town who went to the public schools were off-limits. They were worldly and would tempt me to sin. My choice of friends was easy, as my parents made it for me.

I had a few friends, but not many. There were only a couple of other boys my age at school. I hung out with them occasionally, but I wouldn't call them friends. I didn't fit in with them. They loved to roughhouse and play sports. Especially baseball and football. Hockey was also popular in the winter. I sometimes joined when I was bored, or if my mom pushed me to. Usually the latter. She always worried that I was a loner and didn't have many friends.

It was true. I preferred to be alone. I loved nothing more than to sit on the sofa with a good fantasy book. Or a language book. I recently took an interest in studying foreign languages. My grandparents were Dutch immigrants, so I had been learning Dutch for over a year, and I was getting pretty good at it too. I planned to travel to the Netherlands soon to visit our relatives.

The next language that I started was Japanese. I chose it because I watched lots of anime when my parents weren't home. I was fortunate that they worked full time, and they often left me to babysit.

Anyway, sometimes my mom insisted on me playing with the other boys. I wasn't fond of sports, nor was I interested in talking about the different girls they fancied, or hearing them go on about the latest action movie. Unless it was anime, I didn't care.

When I met Ricky, we connected instantly. He was more international than the other kids were. His family introduced me to all kinds of foods. My family ate bread and potatoes daily, so the only time I had the chance to try something more interesting was when I went to his house. Ricky's mom would make rice and fried noodles, as well as various other types of Filipino dishes. My favorite by a long shot was pork adobo. It was absolutely to die for.

Ricky also liked the same kinds of anime as me, but his parents weren't as strict, so whenever I was at his house, we could watch what we liked. And he started studying Japanese with me as well. It was fun to have a study partner. His family even taught me the occasional Tagalog word. I told myself that would be my next language. Ricky's family even promised to take me to the Philippines the next time they go home for a visit.

"Hey, you okay?" he asked me. That's another thing that made him stand out. He always had a selfless concern for others.

"Yea, I'm fine," I said with a sigh. "I just can't wait for this to be over with."

Seeing his warm smile was the only good thing that could happen today. As I finished tidying my desk, I placed my backpack under my cubicle. Ms. Anderson walked up to me. She was a young lady, maybe in her 30s. She was petite and wore a black ankle-length skirt with a maroon blouse. She usually was in high spirits, but today, she had a stern expression on her face.

"Good Morning Jeremiah. How are you today?"

The idle pleasantries were making this worse. "I'm fine," I muttered.

"Are you ready?" she asked me. "You can follow me upstairs now."

I swallowed hard and gave Ricky one last glance as I followed her up the stairs. My feet dragged on the carpeted floor as I walked behind her. It seemed like an eternity by the time we reached the top of the stairs, and she pushed open the doors into the spacious church sanctuary.

I saw my dad and Mr. Johnson were sitting in the front pew chatting. There was a church function coming up, and they were discussing the details.

They both stood up as they saw us enter. Mr. Johnson picked up a large Bible that had been sitting beside him, and he ushered me to step up in front of the podium.

I followed his direction and took my place where he indicated. We waited for a moment before I heard footsteps. The other students were making their way into the sanctuary. When a student got punished, it was usually by corporal punishment. If it was deemed a severe crime, then it was made public for the entire student body. They thought that would deter further rule breaking. And the rules were plentiful.

Every so often, one girl would get punished for modifying their uniform, usually by shortening their skirts a little. The skirts were expected to be ankle length.

Or sometimes a couple of kids would horse around and break the sacred *"6-inch rule"*. Physical contact was strictly forbidden, especially between the opposite sexes, but it was not allowed between the same sex as well. In their rule book, there was an entire chapter about maintaining proper conduct between the opposite sexes and avoiding any physical contact among the students.

But the public punishment that I was about to go through was reserved for the more serious offenses. *What did I do?* The crime was cheating.

We completed our activity packs independently in our school system, and then we asked permission to score our work. By score, I mean we'd go to the *"Scoring station,"* take the Answer Key, and check our work. Any mistakes, and we would mark it with a red pen, return to our desk, and do the questions again until we got it right.

I was having trouble with a math problem. I asked for help, but no one could explain to me what I was doing wrong. So, on my third attempt at scoring, I just made a small red mark to indicate the answer. But I got caught. It was Mrs. Spark, an older lady who was stern and emotionless. She took me to Mr. Johnson right away and wouldn't listen to my protests about how no one could help me.

They immediately notified my parents and set the date for my punishment. So now, here we were. My father stood to the side, watching with folded arms.

Mr. Johnson waited for everyone to take a seat before he spoke. He addressed his seated audience with a deep voice. "Today, we want to have a serious discussion about the importance of following rules in order to live a Godly life. Everything we do must reflect a life that is pleasing to God."

He paused for a moment to let everyone take in what he said. The entire auditorium was dead silent. Mr. Johnson opened up his Bible to a bookmarked page.

"Now no chastening for the present seemeth to be joyous, but grievous: nevertheless, afterward it yieldeth the peaceable fruit of righteousness unto them which are exercised thereby."

At our school, the only Bible that was allowed was the King James Version, published in 1611. It was the cornerstone of our Baptist community. The Bible could not be read in modern English. Our church leadership considered newer translations to be too soft and conformed too much to the modern world.

Mr. Johnson continued speaking. "What we can take from this passage is that we are to correct those who go astray. It is painful and not pleasant at first, but it is necessary for proper correction. As you go about your day today, remember to always uphold yourself in a way that is pleasing to our Heavenly Father. That is to be our witness as we go about our life among non-believers in our community."

He let that resonate with the captive audience, and he indicated for me to bend over a small table that sat behind the podium. Ms. Anderson put her hands on mine as Mr. Johnson stood behind me. He held in his right hand a ping-pong paddle. He raised it high above his head, paused for a moment, then brought it down. It landed with a swift *thud.* I winced, but kept myself from letting out an audible yell. Ms. Anderson clasped my hands. I remembered my dad's words about taking this graciously. I didn't want my punishment at home to get even worse than it needed to be, so I gritted my teeth and held back the tears.

He gave me two more smacks on my backside and then stopped. I waited for a few moments, but nothing more happened. I stood up straight and looked up at Mr. Johnson, who looked me straight in the eyes.

He laid his hand on my shoulder and said a prayer. I wasn't paying much attention to the words, but it was something about how God would lead me to the path of righteousness from here on out. I didn't care. I felt an immense wave of shame and embarrassment flood over me. I could feel my face getting warm, and so I just looked down at my feet.

To make things worse, when the prayer was over, Ms. Anderson walked up and gave me a tight hug. In this sort of situation, that was acceptable, I guess. She whispered in my ear, "We still love you and hope that this helps you to make better decisions in the future."

I gritted my teeth. This just added to my humiliation. Telling me they love me after whacking me on the ass in front of the entire school? There was something seriously wrong with that picture.

I was ready to get out of there. To hide my face from everyone. To avoid the looks and comments that were sure to come. But not my luck. Mr. Johnson led the group in a round of *Amazing Grace.* When the song finished, the school was dismissed, and everyone headed back downstairs to the Learning Center. Only Mr. Johnson and my father stayed behind. I wasn't sure what I should do, so I just stood to the side quietly. My face was still warm.

My dad signed some papers regarding school disciplinary action. It was only when he finished that I was dismissed and allowed to join my classmates.

I held back the tears as I took a seat at my desk. Ricky's was three desks over. He tried to get my attention, but I ignored him. I felt dizzy and my head throbbed. I didn't want to talk to anyone. I just stared down at my work, unable to concentrate. Within five minutes, my train of thought was interrupted as they called us to stand at attention.

Every morning we started our day by reciting the Pledge of Allegiance to both the American Flag and the Christian Flag. We were taught that patriotism was almost as important of a trait as our commitment to our faith. It went to God, country, and family. In that order.

"I pledge allegiance to the Flag of the United States of America, and to the Republic for which it stands, one Nation under God, indivisible, with liberty and justice for all."

I mumbled the words. We did this often enough that most students just followed along like robots. The words didn't mean anything anymore. Add that to how today was going, and this ritual was unbearable. I just wanted to sit down and hide my face from everyone.

The pledges were followed by a Bible Reading, again in the King James Version, which was a source of irritation for me. But I kept my thoughts to myself and unenthusiastically followed along. Finally, we sang a hymn. We could then sit down, and our school day officially began.

I opened my math pack and glanced at my school planner to see which pages I should work on today. Unlike a traditional school, we worked on individual work packs. We had one for each subject. We'd complete twelve during the school year. We did a few pages each day and then went to the Scoring Station to check our work. That was where I got into trouble the last time.

Our school didn't employ trained teachers. Parents volunteered as school monitors. They checked our work and ensured that we understood the material. From my experience, they didn't always know what they were doing. It was getting more apparent now that I was doing material at a higher level.

When we finished the activity packs, they gave us a test to do. If we got less than 88%, we had to redo our entire pack, regardless of what area we needed to improve on. I'd been begging my parents for the past year to allow me to go to the public school, but they wouldn't budge. They worried I would get into trouble with those *secular kids*. For now, I've accepted this as my lot in life, much to my chagrin.

Finally, the lunch bell rang. I stared at the same math page for half an hour, and I still didn't get it. I was glad for the chance to give my eyes a break.

I took my lunch out of my backpack, and Ricky joined me at the far corner of the lunchroom. This was the usual spot where we ate together.

"How are you feeling?" he asked me as I opened my box of ham and cheese sandwiches.

"I'm fine," I replied as I took a bite. I wasn't feeling very hungry. I set my sandwich back down and looked over at Ricky.

"I'm tired. I want to go home," I said.

Ricky took a side glance to make sure that no one was within earshot. "I told my mom what was happening today. She wasn't too happy. They want to send me to a different school. My mom couldn't believe that they still use the paddle. That's been illegal in the Philippines for years now. It's ridiculous."

"Where will you go?" I asked him. "If you leave, then I'll have nobody."

"We're not sure," he replied. "The reason we're here is that my parents wanted me to get a Christian education. There aren't many options in a small town like this."

I looked down at my food. Today was already turning out to be the worst day of my life, and now my best friend was talking about leaving me. *My best friend?* It was the first time that I've thought of Ricky that way. *But why not?* I didn't have many other friends. At least no one that I could talk to honestly.

But there was something more between us. I thought about him constantly. I enjoyed my time with him. And when we weren't together, I wished we were. He was also super cute. He had these adorable dimples when he smiled. And his dark hair and eyes made him look so handsome. The fact that he loved the same kind of anime as me was another benefit.

I often went to his house on the weekends. The only reason my parents allowed that was because they assumed his family was as conservative as we were since they attended the same church and school. But his family was much more open-minded and, above all, just more fun. They understood that your recreational activities didn't have to revolve solely around the church.

I constantly wanted to be with him. But was it more? Was I developing a crush? No, I couldn't be. If there was anything, I knew it was that homosexuality was one of the worst sins out there. That was something that even Ricky's more laid-back parents wouldn't approve of.

It couldn't be like that. There was no way I was gay. I was overthinking things. I was going to marry a woman and have children one day, right? I simply enjoyed the companionship of my only friend. That was it. Nothing more. So, I dismissed these thoughts.

I took a few more bites of my sandwich before putting it back in my lunch box. "Aren't you going to eat?" Ricky asked me.

"Naw, I'm not hungry," I replied. "I'm going for a walk. I need to clear my head. I'll see you soon."

I enjoyed my time with him, but my head was swimming. Today was a horrible day and there was no sign of it improving. I put my food back in my backpack and pulled out a book I brought from home. I had been reading a British fantasy novel that I borrowed from the library, but I knew I couldn't bring something like that to school. They had a strict policy against anything secular. Especially if they deemed it to be full of the occult. Instead, I brought my self-study Japanese book.

Technically not Christian, but not Occultic either. And it was educational. A couple of the teachers encouraged me to continue studying foreign languages. They often pointed out how maybe God's calling for me was to be a missionary. Actually, that wouldn't be the case. I just liked to watch anime and wanted to enjoy it in its original language. On top of that, I was planning to move to Japan after graduation. The more distance I could put between my small conservative town, the better.

I went upstairs and found a quiet place at the back of the sanctuary to sit down. I opened my book and went over example sentences on how to differentiate the two topic markers that the Japanese use. I read and looked over the example sentences for a couple of minutes before I looked up. I was having a hard time concentrating.

I shut the book and placed it on the bench beside me as I sat there in silence. I looked up at the giant cross on the far wall behind the pulpit.

My thoughts were so muddled. What was true? What wasn't? I wasn't giving up my faith, but the way the church and school portrayed it couldn't be the entirety of what Christianity was about.

My entire life, I was taught that the outside world was evil. We were to remain separate from the secular world. I couldn't have friends from outside our school and church. My parents heavily scrutinized my movie and music choices, especially my mother. I was able to sneak some books from the library past her. Still, for the most part, she had stringent standards for what was allowed and often supervised my library visits as well.

In my social studies packs, I was learning about apartheid in South Africa, and I read that it wasn't as bad as the media would have us believe. Apartheid allowed South Africa to develop much better than what black South Africans would have been able to do if they had done it independently. I then took out a book from the library on this topic. It made me even more confused. Which version was correct? Could our school be pushing a racist narrative in favor of a pro-colonialist one?

And the way we reacted to certain *sins* baffled me. My family had recently cut off contact with my mom's cousin after he came out as gay and brought his partner to a family event. I was still conflicted over the question of homosexuality. But even if we agreed it was wrong, was cutting off a gay family member the correct response?

I held my head in my hands. I was getting a migraine between the events today and now my conflicted feelings regarding my faith. I just wanted to go home, go to bed, and forget about everything going on. I was only fourteen. It seemed like forever until I could leave all of this behind and go my own way.

The bell then rang, announcing the end of lunch. I waited a moment before I picked my book up and headed back downstairs.

CHAPTER 2

My mom picked us up when school ended at four o'clock. I still hadn't finished my math problems, so I took them home for homework. I had two pages to do, and I was probably going to spend the rest of the evening staring at it.

No one spoke during the drive home. My mom finished her shift at the hospital and still wore her scrubs. She drove an eight-passenger minivan. There were four of us who went to school. My two youngest siblings were too young, and so they stayed with our grandparents while we were at school. We took a slight side trip to stop at the farm and pick them up.

The atmosphere was tense, and I couldn't wait to get home. I thought about pulling out my Japanese study book, but I knew I wouldn't be able to concentrate, anyway.

Upon arriving at home, I helped my mom to unload the groceries, and then I was sent to shovel the walk. Just another reminder that I couldn't wait to move away. We had a one-acre yard, and the sidewalk leading up to the front door was pretty long. I think it was an extra measure of punishment, but I had to shovel the driveway as well.

The soft snow that had been falling in the early morning was now packed and hard. I had to grab the sidewalk scraper from the shed. What I hated even more than shoveling snow was having to break up the ice. I would put all my weight behind the scraper and ram it hard into the ice. I did that for five or ten minutes at a time, and then grabbed the shovel and tossed the ice chunks to the side.

After an hour, I was finished. I put the shovel and sidewalk scraper back in the shed and I made my way to the house. It was almost 6:00 pm and already dark outside. My shoulder ached. I stopped for a moment and took in the brisk, cold air. Christmas was only about a week away, and I could see the decorative lights on the neighbor's houses in the distance. As much as I hated winter, I enjoyed Christmas. Or at least the cozy atmosphere that came with it.

We only had another week of school before we were on holiday. Part of me was glad, but that also meant that I wouldn't be able to see Ricky much until we were back at school. I still felt conflicted about these thoughts. Why did I keep thinking about him like this? It was simple. He was my only friend. And being with him helped me to forget the stifling environment that I had at home. That was it. I wasn't feeling romantic thoughts about him. I knew better than that.

Shaking my head, I went inside and took off my mittens, which were soaked through by this point. I kicked off my boots and pushed down my snow pants before hanging up my coat.

I could smell dinner. My mom had the knack for being able to use almost anything to make a savory stew. Today was beef, cabbage, and potatoes. I was famished, but I was still wearing my school uniform. It was soaked with sweat, and it was uncomfortable.

I went straight to my bedroom, where I stripped down and threw my uniform in the laundry basket. I was lucky. Maybe it was something about being the oldest, but I had my own bedroom, which also had an ensuite bathroom and shower. The only room other than the master bedroom that had that.

We had two other bedrooms that were shared by my other siblings. But if my mom had any more kids, I feared I would soon lose the privilege of having my own room. But for now, I was going to enjoy it.

I went into the bathroom and turned on the hot water in the shower. I let it run for a couple of minutes while I laid out my clothes for the evening. It felt so lovely when I finally stepped into the shower. If I had to put up with winter, then my favorite part was going to be coming in from the bitter cold and taking a hot shower.

It wasn't hot enough until the entire bathroom filled with

steam. I took a deep breath. *Enjoy it while you can,* I told myself. I knew I wasn't out of the woods yet. I was still in trouble. Despite the public punishment at school, I still hadn't heard the last of it.

After ten minutes, I turned off the water and stepped out of the shower. After drying off, I put on a pair of cotton shorts and a T-shirt. I then took another deep breath and made my way to the dining room.

My sister, Mary, sat at the table. Our dad had just woken. He was going to join us for dinner before showering and heading off to work.

With dinner laid out on the table, everyone took their seats, with dad at the head of the table and our mom at the opposite end. I sat on my dad's left side. The boys sat on one side while the girls on the other side.

We all joined hands, closed our eyes, and bowed our heads as dad said grace. He said his usual prayer. He thanked God for the day, that He had kept everyone safe, that He had given us many blessings. He further thanked God for the food and asked Him to bless the hands that had prepared it. And finally, had added something new. He thanked God that, despite all of our failings, He still loved us. He asked God to further guide our paths and help us to walk righteously. I knew this was directed at me, and my gut twisted into knots while I listened to that.

Finally, he asked God to keep him safe while he was at work and said *Amen*. That was the signal that we could dig in. As I helped myself to a heaping helping of mixed vegetables while waiting for someone to pass the pot of stew down, my dad spoke to me. I braced myself for what was to come.

"So, I've talked it over with your mom, and you're grounded for the next three weeks."

I let out an audible gasp. "But, why? Wasn't what I had at school enough?"

"We did consider that, and we're proud of how well you handled it, which is why we're only grounding you for a couple of weeks." He glanced at my mom. "We had been talking about two months."

I poked around in my food with my fork. I had nothing to say. "And you'll have extra chores at home," my dad continued. "If you complain, then we'll extend it."

I felt a retort welling up inside me, but I bit my tongue. I knew better than to shoot myself in the foot, so I just stared at my food and nodded.

"What was that?" my dad asked me. "I didn't hear you."

"Yes, sir," I said through gritted teeth. *Could this get any worse?*

My mom then joined in. "That goes for your library privileges, too. No visits to the library until after New Year. That includes going to use the internet."

We didn't have the internet at home, so the library was the only place where I could access it. I'd check my emails, surf the web, or look for resources to help with my language studies. This really upset me, but I didn't dare to argue. I knew that the case was closed.

I ate my dinner without saying a word. As good as it was, I didn't help myself to seconds, as was the norm, but excused myself and went to my bedroom to do my homework.

I took a seat at my desk and pulled out my math pack. I was getting a headache already thinking about it. My parents usually weren't much help with this, so I was on my own to figure it out.

I stared at the problems for a few minutes. I wish Ricky was here with me. He was brilliant with academics. While I excelled in English, he did well in math and science. Some of the other kids at school teased him that it was because he was Asian, but I knew better. He was just naturally bright and actually enjoyed this stuff.

I never asked him to help me, but maybe I should. Not because I wanted to figure this out, but because I wanted to be with him. *There it was again?* I always wished to be with him. *Was I that lonely? Or was I developing a crush on him?*

I shook my head to rid myself of the idea. I just wanted to finish this homework so I could go to bed. I was grounded for the next three weeks anyway, so I didn't have much to look forward to.

I wasn't sure how much time passed, but when I opened my

eyes, I saw him. Ricky's face was only six inches from mine. *What was he doing in my room?*

That's when I noticed something. I wasn't in my room. I surveyed my surroundings, but I couldn't make sense of things. I didn't recognize where I was.

I looked back at Ricky. He didn't say anything. He was just smiling at me. I wasn't sure what to ask first.

"What are you doing here?" I got out. He didn't reply right away, but just kept smiling. I loved that smile of his.

"Aren't you happy to see me?" he eventually asked.

"Yes, I am. But what are you doing here?" I looked around again. "Where is here anyway?"

He reached his hand out to me. "Come. Let me show you something."

I took his hand and stood from where I sat at my desk. I took another look around and realized that I was in my room, after all. It was shrouded in dark shadows and was unrecognizable. I stood up and followed Ricky out of my room. He didn't let go of my hand, and I didn't protest.

We walked out into the living room. A couple of my younger siblings were at the kitchen table, working on their homework. My dad was putting on his boots to head out to work, and my mom was sitting on the sofa watching the evening news while doing some crocheting. The youngest kids were at her feet, playing with their toys.

No one seemed to take notice of us as we walked towards the front door. They definitely hadn't let my friend come over. Especially as I was grounded. This didn't make much sense.

I attempted to grab my jacket, but Ricky just kept pulling me along. "You won't need that," he said to me with a smile.

As soon as we set foot outside, I realized what he meant. Despite it being dark and the snow covering the yard, it didn't feel cold at all. I felt as if we were still in my room.

We stepped onto the sidewalk and under our feet came the crunching sound as we walked over a layer of freshly fallen snow. We continued to the driveway. I saw the lights of my dad's truck, which was running in order to warm up. We just enjoyed the quiet and serenity of everything until I heard the front door. My dad came walking up to the driveway. I was trying to think of what to say to him, but he didn't even look at me. He stepped into his truck, and a moment later, he backed out of the driveway and headed off down the gravel road.

We stood there for a few more minutes until the garage's motion detector lights went out. I heard Ricky's breathing, and I'm sure that he heard mine as well. Other than that, it was dead silent except for the faint sound of the falling snow. If you strained your ears, you could hear the ever so soft rhythm as the snowflakes softly touched down one by one.

I realized our hands came apart by this point. I looked at Ricky. It was just the two of us among the falling snow. Either way you looked, there was darkness. The nearest house was about half a kilometer down the road. If you looked carefully, you could see their Christmas lights in the distance. Other than a couple of far-off houses, it was a tree-lined gravel road with the only light provided by the moon.

We turned left and walked down the road. I didn't have time to put on my shoes either. But when I remembered that, I realized my feet were neither wet nor cold. I looked down at my feet. It was like I was weightless. My feet touched the snow ever so slightly as I walked, but didn't make an imprint.

We walked for about ten minutes before we came across a small park bench. I scratched my head. We were on an isolated country road with not a park in sight, but I shrugged it off, and we took a seat.

Our eyes met, and Ricky spoke first. "I'm sorry about what happened at school," he said to me. "It was horrible what they did to you today."

I shrugged. "It's fine, I guess. I wish I hadn't gotten grounded, though." I said. "So, once the school break begins, I guess I won't see you until the New Year."

I turned away and starred at the ground. I could feel myself going red. I still couldn't understand what was going on. This felt surreal. But it was just Ricky and me, so I didn't have anything to complain about.

"There'll still be church," he reminded me. "Aren't you going to the Christmas service?"

How could I forget? Christmas Day Service. New Year's Service. Our whole life revolved around the church. At least we'd still see each other, albeit briefly.

"I forgot. Of course, we'll be there." I looked him in the eyes and smiled. I didn't know what to say. "What are your plans for Christmas?" I asked him.

"We'll stay home. We have some relatives coming to visit from out of town. We might take them around to see the lights. And of course, we'll have a party on New Year's Eve. I was hoping to invite you."

Ugh, just what I needed. Another reminder. This was going to be a horrible Christmas. We sat there in silence. I wasn't sure what to say. I felt all kinds of mixed feelings. A part of me felt happy. Finally, the two of us were out here enjoying some quality time together. But it also felt strained, knowing that for the next couple of weeks I'd be spending my holiday at home while he was out having fun.

"So, you said that you wanted to show me something?" I asked. I just remembered that.

"Just wait. You'll see soon," he replied as he looked up at the sky. I followed his gaze.

It was a beautiful night. The sky was clear, and we could see the stars clearly. In science, I was studying the constellations. I tried to figure out how many I could identify. Unfortunately, I could only recognize the *Big Dipper*. I pointed it out to Ricky. I wanted to show off my knowledge a little bit.

"Yes, I see," he replied. "And that there is *Taurus*. And that one up there is *Gemini*."

He was the one showing off. I noticed he scooted a little closer. He leaned into me as he pointed out the star formations in the sky. I could almost feel his breath on my cheek. It felt like a dream. This couldn't be real. I rested my head on his shoulder. He didn't budge, but shifted to accommodate me.

I heard him whisper in my ear. "There it is."

I looked up at him. "Huh?"

"There," and he pointed up at the sky. "That's what I wanted to show you."

What I saw almost took my breath away. At first, I saw an object streak across the sky. It was gleaming. A shooting star? Then I saw another one. And another.

"Isn't it beautiful?" Ricky whispered in my ear.

These weren't shooting stars. It was a meteor shower. The first one I'd ever seen firsthand. It was breathtaking. I watched with my jaw open.

It went on for over five minutes before subsiding. Even after it was over, I couldn't get over what I just saw. It was amazing.

"Wow, that was spectacular," I remarked. Ricky nodded in agreement.

I glanced at my watch. "I should probably get home before I get into even more trouble than I'm already in."

Ricky just nodded in agreement as we stood up and headed back to my house.

We walked for a few minutes, and I felt my hand once again meeting his. Our fingers became intertwined. I took in the warmth of his hands, but suddenly I became self-conscious of mine. I hoped my hand wasn't too sweaty. If that was the case, he didn't seem to notice.

The walk back home went by too quickly, and before I knew it, we were standing in front of my driveway. The motion sensor light on the garage flicked on as if to announce our arrival.

Most of the lights in the house were off except for a small lamp in the living room. That would be my mom sitting in her chair watching the evening news. She was probably waiting for me to come home.

I turned back to Ricky. "Thanks for tonight. It was fun."

He smiled back at me. "I had fun too."

"How are you getting back home?" I asked him. "Do you need a ride?"

"It's fine," he said. "I can make it back home just fine."

"Ok," I said as he turned to look at my house. "Well, I guess I'd better go. Thanks again."

"Wait!" he said as he grabbed my arm and I turned back to face him. "I wanted to give you something before you go." He then leaned into me. I realized what was happening and didn't resist. I closed my eyes and I felt our lips meet. His lips were warm. Warm and moist. We maintained contact for about fifteen seconds before breaking apart.

I licked my lips, and I could taste him. Our eyes remained locked on each other for a moment before I turned and walked back towards my house.

"Jeremiah!" I heard someone shouting. A sharp knocking sound followed. And then more shouting. I jerked back. I was at my desk in my room. My eyes felt heavy. I wiped my face with my sleeve.

"What?" I called out.

It was my mom. "For the third time, the phone's for you."

I got up and opened the door to see my mom holding the phone as far as the cord would allow.

"It's Ricky," she told me.

Ricky? On the phone for me?

"Remember that you're grounded. This is the only call you're allowed to take. Tell him no phone calls until after the New Year."

Still feeling groggy, I took the receiver from her.

"Hello? Ricky?"

It was so soothing to hear his voice on the other end of the receiver. "Hey, how are you?"

I had a weird feeling in my stomach. Wasn't he just here a few moments ago?

I glanced at my mom, who resumed her spot on the sofa with her crocheting. She was out of earshot. I felt confused. I looked at my watch. It was only 8:30.

His voice was still coming from the other end. "Are you still there?"

I shook the sleep out of my eyes again. "Yea, I'm here. Sorry."

"I just wanted to check if you were okay after today. Did you get in trouble at home too?"

"Yea, kind of," I replied. "I'm grounded and was told to tell you we can't talk until after the school break."

There was a moment of silence. I realized the kiss hadn't been real. He wasn't here. I was dreaming. Or fantasizing, maybe? I gave a side glance to my mom, who was preoccupied with her crocheting. I had to tell him. I lowered my voice to a barely audible whisper, "Ricky, I have to tell you something." I swallowed hard. *I'm gay?* How could I just blurt it out? But I felt I had to tell him. Instead, what came out of my mouth was, "I need to talk to you tomorrow."

Ricky sat across from me at the lunch table. I felt like I had enormous bags under my eyes. I was up most of the night, unable to sleep.

I ate my ham and cheese sandwich as Ricky ate his packed lunch of white rice and some grilled meat.

"So, what was it you wanted to tell me?" he asked me between bites. I looked around the lunch area. Most of the students appeared to be out of earshot, but it was too big of a risk.

"Finish up, and let's go talk upstairs," I told him. "I don't want to say anything down here."

He shrugged and continued eating. I took the last couple of bites of my sandwich and laid my head down on my arms. I was getting a nasty headache. Not sure if it was from stress or just my nerves.

Ricky shook me awake a few minutes later. He was finished eating, and we took a stroll upstairs. We entered the church sanctuary and took a seat in a pew. I enjoyed the quietness of this space—a pleasant change from the activity I was used to on Sunday mornings.

I wasn't sure how to start this conversation. "I dreamt about you last night."

He just looked at me. I wished that he'd say something.

"You came to my house. You took me for a walk, and we sat

down on a park bench and watched a meteor shower."

"A park bench? By your house?"

"I said that it was a dream."

I wasn't sure how to continue. *Should I just blurt it out?*

"I think I'm…" I couldn't get the words out. My eyes met his. He had a quizzical look written all over his face.

I took a deep breath before I continued. But I still couldn't find the words to say what I wanted to say. "I really like you."

There. I said it. I grimaced as I waited for his reply. He just looked blankly back at me. He blinked a couple of times and kept staring at me. I couldn't take the tension.

"I mean, not romantically," I blurted. "I just mean that I've been very lonely. I have a hard time making friends. I don't get along with any of the kids here either." I wished he would say something. "I'm thrilled that you moved here, and I've never felt as close with anybody else as I do with you."

I waited for an eternity for him to reply. "It's fine. I feel the same way about you," he said. The tightness in my chest loosened a little. "It was a big change for me when we moved all the way here. I still remember when I met you a few months ago. I still had a hard time speaking English and hadn't made any friends yet. You were the only one who took the time to make me feel welcome."

I diverted my eyes before they welled up with tears. A warm sensation filled me. It started in my chest and resonated outwards. "You're my best friend Jeremiah, and I will never forget your kindness."

"You're my best friend too," I whispered back, and I laid my head on his shoulder. It was just like in my dream. Maybe things wouldn't be that bad after all.

The sound of the main door creaking open reached my ears. As fast as I could, I pushed myself away from Ricky and spun around. Mr. Johnson stood in the doorway. I forgot that his office was just outside those doors.

"What are you boys up to?" he demanded.

CHAPTER 3

As a kid, my favorite activity by far was Bible Camp. Every summer, I'd go for an entire week. It was the only time I was away from home and my family. The campsite was located in a small village that mainly consisted of summer cottages.

It sat on the edge of a large lake. Many of the neighbors went out with their speed boats or did some fishing and swimming. It was a beautiful location to get away from your daily life.

I have memories of one summer in particular. This was the last time I've been to that camp. The reason that I haven't been back since will be explained shortly. This happened two years earlier, when I was twelve.

The camp was always in July. Some things were the same as my home and school. For example, we had to read the Bible in the King James Version. Contact between the opposite sexes was highly discouraged. Clothing had to be modest. No short shorts. Nothing that allowed one's underwear to be visible was permitted. And specific rules for the girls included things like no tank tops, jewelry, make-up, or one-piece swimwear.

It was also strictly forbidden to bring non-Christian material to the camp. So, other than my Bible, I couldn't bring any other books with me, except for a notebook which I used to keep an account of my week's adventures.

I couldn't wait as I sat beside my mom on the almost one-hour trip to the camp. A couple of my siblings went as well, but on a different week. They divided us up by age groups, and I went to the one intended for ages ten to fourteen.

Lots of people were out on their quads, and the lake was busy with people in speedboats as we drove past the lake. To access the lake from the campsite, we had to walk about a mile through a tree-lined path. Usually, we went once a day to go out on the barge, which was a large boat that had a second level with a diving board. It would take us out into the middle of the lake, where we would spend the afternoon swimming. I was a strong swimmer, and I always had a lot of fun.

We pulled into the camp's parking lot and headed down to the Registration Office. I bumped into Elijah, one of the Camp Director's children. He was about my age. Very friendly but overly obsessed with science, and I found him to be socially awkward. He was friendly enough, though, and he greeted me warmly. It was always great to see old faces. People that I only ever saw once a year.

I was an introvert and didn't do well in new situations. The most challenging part about the camp was that there were always new kids every year. So, I bonded with those whom I got to see each time.

Stepping into the Registration Office, Elijah's sister, Ruth—who was a few years older than me—greeted us. I think she would have been about sixteen at the time. And their mother, Mrs. Campbell, was there with her. Both of them wore plain jean skirts that extended to their ankles. They were very strict in their beliefs about modesty. Even though the camp rules didn't dictate that girls had to wear skirts, this family, who had ten children of their own, required it of their daughter as they believed pants were too masculine.

Many of the families from the same social circle believed the same. But the camp was meant as a community outreach, and most of the camp attendees came from non-Christian families. And so, the Campbells didn't strictly enforce some of their more fundamental ideas.

This was one of the only times where I could interact with secular kids. But my family, and the other Christian families, expected that we didn't build close friendships with any of the secular kids unless they came to know Christ.

Upon receiving our payment receipt and the information packet which told us which cabin I was staying in, we went back to the van and took out my duffel bag and my bedding.

My cabin was at the far edge of the campsite. It stood only a couple of feet from where the trees began. It was like being on the edge of a dark forest. The whole section of about ten cabins was for the boys. The girls' cabins were on the other side, closer to the parking lot and the mess hall.

As I stepped into the wooden cabin, I saw a couple of other boys getting their beds set up. I immediately recognized Daniel. He was my cabin mate last year. He ran over and gave me a high five and a pat on the back. I was glad that I was sharing accommodations with one person I already knew.

We were then introduced to our cabin counselor, a young man by the name of Philip. I gauged him to be about twenty years old. He was new to the camp, as I knew all the returning counselors. He was handsome and fit, with a little bit of stubble underneath his chin.

After saying goodbye to my mom, I got settled in. There were eleven other boys my age, Philip and a junior counselor, who looked to be about seventeen or eighteen.

It was a rowdy bunch, but they seemed like they would be fun to spend the week with. If I remember correctly, Daniel was into the same TV shows I was, and we used to talk about those. His family wasn't very strict, and sometimes he would smuggle in some comic books or trading cards.

As evening approached, we assembled in the chapel for songs and devotions. It was always a lot of fun. The songs were very fast-paced, and most of them were action songs. By the time we could sit down, we felt like we'd been working out for some time already.

Mr. Campbell then walked up to the front of the chapel. He was very tall and slim and sported a nice brown beard. He was the director of the camp, and despite having views of the Bible that were quite outdated, he was very nice and intelligent. He consistently demonstrated amazing science experiments that ensured he had everyone's attention.

Today he showed us some dinosaur fossils. He explained to us how they couldn't be millions of years old. Apparently, the public schools were teaching evolution in order to deceive us. At that time, I wholeheartedly believed what he taught us, as I hadn't been exposed to any contrasting ideas. Finally, we ended with a Bible reading and prayer before being dismissed to go for dinner.

Daniel and I ran down the hill to the mess hall and met up with the rest of the boys from our cabin. We went in and helped ourselves to mashed potatoes and roast beef, followed by jello and whipped cream. My mom's cooking was pretty good, but the camp's food was absolutely to die for.

After we ate, we grabbed our clothes and headed to the showers. This was the one part of my time at the camp that I dreaded. As a kid, I was always told that our bodies were something to hide and be ashamed of, but most of the kids who didn't go to church didn't seem to care. They ran around the shower room stark naked and without any sense of embarrassment. They were hitting each other with their towels and tackling one another to the ground.

I was always timid and would wrap my towel tight around my waist as I walked to the shower stall, but the other boys would laugh at me. They told me we all have the same parts, so there's nothing to be shy about. This was always a source of embarrassment for me, and because of this, I hated taking a shower at camp.

On this particular occasion, one of the boys pulled my towel off of me, and they all burst out into laughter as I placed my hand over my groin and made a dash for the shower stall.

I showered quickly, and Daniel, who showered in the adjoining cubicle, was kind enough to lend me his towel so that I could dry off and stealthily conceal myself as I pulled my underwear back on. The other boys continued to point and guffaw.

After making our way back to the cabin, I went straight to bed. I was on the top bunk, and Daniel was on the one beside me, allowing us to chit chat a bit before lights out.

I usually had a hard time falling asleep away from home, but this time I was exhausted, and everything went black as soon as my head touched my pillow.

I didn't remember anything until I woke up, what seemed like mere moments later. It was pitch black, and I could hear the faint snoring of my cabin mates. I ducked my head underneath the covers to illuminate my watch. It read 3:15 AM. It was still the middle of the night, but I could feel the strain on my bladder. I didn't much like the idea of going out in the middle of the night, but I didn't think that I could hold out for another three hours.

I nimbly swung my leg over the side of the bed and descended the rickety ladder. Making as little noise as possible, I stepped onto the floor and crossed to the door, opening and closing it ever so lightly.

The building that housed the toilets and showers wasn't a far walk. Just opposite of the firepit, which was in the clearing immediately outside the cabin. There were also a couple of outside lights that were on and illuminated my path.

I slipped inside, made my way to the urinal, and quickly did my business. It was when I turned to leave that I thought I heard something. It was coming from one of the shower stalls. I slowly and quietly moved towards the source of the sound. I was careful not to even breathe.

I peeked around the corner and I saw a boy from one of the other cabins. I didn't know his name, nor had I interacted much with him, but I was curious what he was up to, and so I kept myself hidden around the corner of the stall.

At first, I wasn't sure what he was doing. He was sitting on the floor, and he had his pants pulled down past his ankle. He had his hand between his legs and was moving it vigorously up and down. I watched for a couple of moments more before realizing that I was witnessing something that I shouldn't. Something taboo.

I turned and dashed for the door, yanking it open and running back to my cabin. I ran as fast as my legs would carry me, not stopping until I reached my destination. I stopped and tried to get my breathing under control before I carefully opened the door and slipped inside.

It wasn't until I was back on my bunk and was snug in my sleeping bag before I processed what I witnessed. I still wasn't sure what I saw. All I knew was that it was something terrible. It was a cardinal sin. I tried to calm down and forget what I saw. As I did so, I slowly drifted off to sleep.

It wasn't until wake-up call at 6:00 AM that I was up again. The memories of last night were pushed to the back of my mind as I jumped out of bed and threw myself down onto the floor. Daniel was already pulling a pair of jeans on. I dug in my bag and pulled out a pair as well. We then ran to the mess hall and enjoyed a hearty breakfast of French toast, breakfast sausages, bacon, and hash browns. It beat the cold cereal I often ate at home. On special occasions, such as Christmas, or someone's birthday, my mom would make pancakes or bacon and eggs. But otherwise, we just helped ourselves to cereal or made ourselves toast. I always looked forward to the meals at camp. Their kitchen always did a great job.

For the rest of the morning, I hung out with a few of the boys. We played basketball and did archery. Afterward, we had a chapel session and lunch before being allowed to go swimming in the afternoon. Swimming was always the highlight of camp for me. Daniel and I were two of the first ones on the barge.

After ten minutes of jumping into the water, getting out, and going back up the diving board, something crossed my mind. Daniel was really cute. I was behind him as we made our way up the ladder to the diving board. I couldn't help but notice how smooth his skin was. The way the water dripped down his tanned back and arms. His medium-length brown hair was something else when soaking wait.

If he turned his head fast, I felt mesmerized by the sight of his wet hair bouncing from side to side. I hadn't thought anything like this the year before, but at that time on the lake, I looked at him every chance I had. I admired his arms. His chest. Even the shape of his behind as he walked ahead of me.

That night, after an exciting and eventful day, I laid in bed, trying to process what I was thinking. I'd never looked at a boy like that before. And deep inside, I knew it was wrong. I shifted onto my stomach, folded my hands in front of me, and I said a silent prayer. I prayed to God to forgive me for all my sins, including any sinful thoughts I might have.

I wasn't sure if God heard me. But I believed that if I was sincere enough, he would. These thoughts comforted me, and I fell asleep.

The rest of the week continued without incident. We did lots more archery, ate plenty of junk food from the tuck shop, and even went on a hiking trip. We were having a great time, and Daniel and I were inseparable.

We could only see each other this one time every year, so we made the best use of our time. His family was Christian as well, but they were more laid back. His parents let him watch almost anything that he wanted. He even showed me his Bible. He was allowed to read it in Modern English. Not like the King James version that I was made to read.

He invited me to come to stay at his house over the summer at some point, but my mom would never allow me. She said that families like his aren't true Christians. My mom used the term lukewarm. She said that they didn't follow the Bible as closely as we were supposed to. So, we were friends during camp, and that was it.

It wasn't until our second to last night at camp that something happened. After our chapel session, we ate Rice Krispie squares, cookies, and hot chocolate while we sat around the campfire and sang worship songs.

This was another part of camp that I enjoyed. I wore a sweater as the evening was chilly, and the hot chocolate hit the right spot.

We were into our third song, and I was belting out the notes at the top of my lungs. It was then that Daniel got up. He said he had to go to the bathroom. I didn't think anything of it, but after a few more songs, he never came back, and I got curious where he had gone off to.

After the singing ended and I had a couple of more cups of hot chocolate, I ran to the bathrooms to check on him and make sure that he was okay.

I entered the building and I called out. "Daniel! Are you in here?"

I didn't get an answer. I walked around and saw that all the stall doors were open. There was no one in the showers as well. I scratched my head. *Where could he have gone?*

I ran to the cabin. Maybe he went back there. Upon arriving at the cabin, I saw that the light was on, and I heard hushed voices. Slowly, I pulled open the door and stepped in. I heard more whispering and the sounds of scuffling.

I saw Daniel sitting on the floor, huddled together with four other boys. They were trying to conceal something by shoving it under the nearest bed. When they saw me, Daniel gave a sigh of relief.

"It's just Jeremiah. He's okay, guys," he told his friends. They all relaxed and pulled the object back from under the bed. It was a magazine.

"What do you guys have there?" I asked curiously as I knelt beside them. I didn't realize what I was looking at right away. But on closer inspection, my eyes grew wide. I never saw anything like this before.

The magazine had various pictures of women. Grown, scantily clad women. Some of them were sitting on motorcycles wearing nothing but a thong or a bikini.

I wasn't sure what to think. There was a part of me that felt guilty. I knew we shouldn't be looking at something like this. But on the other hand, I was curious. I'd never seen a naked female body before. Or even a woman dressed in such a provocative way. We didn't go swimming often, as my mom worried I'd see girls dressed in a way I shouldn't. But we did occasionally go swimming with some other church families. Or while I was at camp. Then all the girls wore conservative one-piece swimsuits.

I didn't even know that swimwear like this existed. It barely covered anything but the bare essentials. The other boys were really excited as they flipped the pages. It was doing something for them. Not for me. I just felt a sense of curiosity. This wouldn't be something that I'd seek out on my own, but I wanted to take a closer look since the boys already had it out.

"Whoa, look at this one!" Daniel exclaimed. He had a pillow over his lap, and I could tell by his facial expression that he was fascinated by what he saw—the same for his other friends.

"Look at the size of this girl's tits!" another boy pointed out. Their voices were getting louder now.

Tits? I never heard that word before. But I saw he was pointing at the girl's breasts. My mom used to breastfeed my younger siblings, but otherwise, I never thought of a girl's breasts in any special way. But these boys were very fascinated by what they saw.

We continued to flip through the magazine for a good ten minutes or so, and the more we did, the more stimulated the other boys seemed to get.

It was while we were on a page of a famous pop singer, who was in various erotic poses while wearing a tight bikini, that the door swung open. The boys scrambled to shove the magazine back under the bed. I quickly got to my feet and tried to look as innocent as I could.

Our camp counselor, Philip, came strolling in. He pushed past the other boys and reached under the bed, pulling out the magazine. He swung around to look at everyone.

"Whose is this?" he demanded. He was met with silence, so he repeated himself. "Whose is this? Who brought this?"

I stared at the floor, hoping that he wouldn't notice me. Out of the corner of my eye, I saw someone move. I looked over. Daniel was holding up his hand. Philip was furious. "Come with me!" he said to Daniel. It was an order, not a request.

He turned to the rest of us. "All of you are to stay here until I'm back. Understood?"

We all nodded, and Philip marched out of the cabin with Daniel close on his heels. I climbed up onto my bunk and laid down. I stared at the ceiling. My heart was pounding in my chest. *Was I going to get into trouble? What were my parents going to say when they find out?* They would be so angry with me. I knew better. I should have just minded my own business.

I felt the tears welling up, and I tried my best to keep them contained, but I couldn't. I rolled over onto my side, and the tears rolled down my face. Camp was the highlight of my summer, and now that was going to get taken away from me as well.

Everything went dark. It seemed like only a few moments later that someone was shaking me.

"Get up and come down here." It was Philip's voice. I slowly rolled over. Philip was standing there with the other boys. I reluctantly pushed back the covers and climbed down the steel ladder.

"Where's Daniel?" I asked.

"He's gone. His parents took him home." Philip replied.

My heart sank.

"As for you guys, you're wanted up at the office," Philip said. We followed him for the ten-minute walk up to the registration building. It was late and dark outside. Most of the kids were in their cabin already. It would be lights out soon.

Mr. Campbell was waiting for us. His face was stern. The five of us sat down on the chairs that he indicated across from him. "Daniel said that he brought that magazine from home. Is that true? No one is covering for him, right?"

We nodded as we looked down in shame.

"You all know our rules on obscene material, right?" We nodded again.

"The next time someone brings something like that here, you are to come and tell us immediately. You don't participate and help try to hide it." All we could do was nod again. No one said anything.

Mr. Campbell then warned us of the dangers of viewing material such as this. How we are to live by God's standards, which included avoiding the presence of evil.

It seemed like forever by the time his speech ended. "Daniel was sent home," he told us. "And if any of you are caught doing something like this again, then so will you. Do you boys understand?"

We nodded one last time. "I will also have a chat with your parents before you guys return home. Now I want you all to shower and go to bed."

"Yes, Mr. Campbell," we muttered as we stood and followed Philip back to our cabin.

I grabbed my pajamas, went to the bathroom, and took a shower. The other boys did so as well, but I couldn't look at them nor speak to them. I felt too ashamed of myself.

I sat in the shower for longer than was necessary as the water ran over my body. I hunched down on the ground and wrapped my arms around my knees. The warm water felt good, but I couldn't care less at this moment. I had so many emotions running through my head.

I dreaded when my mom would come to pick me up. I knew I was going to get into trouble. I should have known better than to join the boys in looking at the magazine. I didn't understand why I did that.

Finally, I turned the water off, got dressed, and brushed my teeth. The other boys must have gone back to the cabin already. I was alone here. I didn't care. I didn't want to see anyone, anyway.

I finished brushing my teeth, threw my towel over my shoulders, and made my way back to the cabin. The lights were off, and everything was quiet when I went inside.

I put my clothes back in my bag as quietly as I could and climbed up onto my bed. I looked over at Daniel's bed, and I felt that tight feeling in my chest again as I realized he wasn't going to come back.

Before I tried to fall asleep, I said a prayer. I asked God to forgive me once again for my sins. I asked him not to send me to hell for what I did that night. The feeling of guilt abated a little, and I drifted off to sleep.

The last day of camp was the longest day I ever experienced. Daniel was my best friend at camp, and I didn't need to hang out with anyone else. I would have spent time with some of the other boys from my cabin, but we were all avoiding each other at this point.

My mom came to pick me up the day after, and as expected, she was furious when she heard what happened.

The drive home seemed to take forever. That night my father took a leather belt and beat my ass until I developed welts. I can't remember ever seeing him that angry in my life. They also grounded me for the duration of the summer holiday. For six whole weeks. It didn't matter that it was the other boys who were into it, and I was just a curious bystander. I tried to use that as an argument but to no avail.

They also forbade me to ever contact those boys again, and I was never allowed back to that camp, or any other camp, for that matter. My parents felt they could no longer trust my judgment, and I was never allowed to spend a night away from home without a relative being present.

CHAPTER 4

Never mind when I got in trouble for cheating, that was nothing compared to how I felt at that moment while we were both sitting in Mr. Johnson's office. Ricky sat across from me, and we didn't dare to even look at each other. Mr. Johnson was on the phone talking to our parents. He asked them to come in immediately for a meeting.

After he finished on the phone, Mr. Johnson turned to us both. "Are you boys ready to tell me what you were up to in there?" he asked. His voice was stern and a little intimidating.

Ricky spoke up. "I told you. We were just sitting there." I sensed a bit of defiance in his tone of voice. I found that impressive. I wasn't that brave. I just cowered and accepted what was coming my way. I might make up an excuse, but in no way would I get confrontational with someone in authority.

It was evident Mr. Johnson didn't believe him. "You know you're not supposed to be in the sanctuary without permission," he said to us.

"It was my fault," I said. "I'm sorry, sir, I forgot. I often go in there when I want to sit and read quietly. It slipped my mind that we weren't allowed to be in there."

"And you forgot about our six-inch rule as well?" he asked. My heart sank. That's what we were in trouble for. It had nothing to do with us being in the sanctuary.

"You know we don't permit our students to be in such close contact with each other," he continued. "That's especially aimed at preventing romantic relationships between boys and girls. We never thought that we'd have to worry about there being problems between two boys." He narrowed his eyes at us. "I'm not making accusations, but you must understand how bad that looks."

I looked at the floor and wished that I could just melt away and disappear.

Ricky's mom, Mrs. Vergara, was the first to arrive. She knocked on the office door before entering.

Mrs. Vergara was short and fairly plump, but she was a sweet lady who could brighten a room by her very presence. She was like a second mom to me when I was at their house. She had a look of confusion on her face as she stepped into the office.

Mr. Johnson explained to her how we had been in the sanctuary alone. How we had our arms around each other. Technically, I just had my head on Ricky's shoulder, but I guess if Mr. Johnson wanted to embellish the story, then so be it.

Mrs. Vergara just laughed it off. "Well, they're best friends. What do you expect? Jeremiah is like family. The boys are practically brothers."

"It breaks our six-inch rule," Mr. Johnson told her. "We don't allow any of our students to have physical contact with each other. That includes public displays of affection. Platonic or... otherwise." He gave us both a very suspicious look as he uttered that last sentence. I cringed in my seat.

"Okay, I will make sure that Ricky knows not to break that rule then," she said. Mrs. Vergara was obtuse to what was being implied. My mom, on the other hand, picked up on it at once. She arrived a few minutes later, and when she heard Mr. Johnson's accusations, she was quick to defend me.

"I can assure you my son is not one of those," she insisted.

"Like what?" Mrs. Vergara asked. She still wasn't aware of the accusation that the principal was making against us. I knew very well, and I hid my face behind my backpack. I was ashamed because even though we hadn't done anything, I knew the accusation was true.

"I will have a talk with him when we get home," my mom promised. Mr. Johnson leaned back in his chair as he thought for a moment.

"The boys didn't do anything inappropriate. And I believe you, that your son knows better than to engage in that sort of behavior." Again, he gave me that look of distrust. "But you have to understand how this could be perceived. If anyone else saw, it would ignite rumors. Not just in the school, but across the entire town. It is a small town, after all. You have to be aware that we can't have that. It would harm your family's reputation. And that of our school and church."

"I fully understand," my mom said in agreement. "I will have a talk with Jeremiah when we get home. I guarantee it won't happen again."

"Okay, I appreciate that," he replied. "The same goes for you, Mrs. Vergara."

"I still don't understand what they did wrong, except breaking the six-inch rule," she replied. "But I'll talk to Ricky and make sure he knows not to break any more school rules."

That seemed reasonable enough for Mr. Johnson, as he nodded, and we were dismissed. I was relieved that we didn't receive any sort of formal punishment. Instead, we suffered the embarrassment of being accused of having done absolutely nothing.

It was still early afternoon, and class was beginning again soon, so we hurried off downstairs. Our mothers waited a while longer to talk with the principal.

We both exchanged a look of relief as we took our seats in the Learning Center. We narrowly avoided getting in trouble. I still had the lingering shame from the last time, which was only the previous day.

The rest of the school day went by quickly, and before I realized it, I was in the van with my mom and younger siblings on our way home. I avoided getting in trouble at school, but I was about to get an earful at home from both my mom and dad.

First, they gave me a ten-minute lecture on the sin of homosexuality. That was one of the worst sins that there was. It was a moral sin that defiled both the body and the soul. My skin was getting all clammy as I stood there and listened. I was very uncomfortable as I sat there and took it—all of this just for sitting there with my friend.

I listened to them recap the Biblical story of Adam and Even for what seemed the millionth time. I was told how God's plan was for one man and one woman and how any deviation from that went against God's will.

They then explained how in today's society, the absolute worst thing for a Christian was to be associated with the evil outside world. And one way to go that path was for there to be rumors about one's sexuality.

They told me they knew I wasn't gay. I was raised in the church, and that gave them the assurance that I knew better. But they warned me I must also be self-aware and consciously not do anything that would get other people in our community to jump to conclusions and start rumors.

That went for the books one read or the clothing they wore. My dad was quick to point out how many of the boys in the anime that I wasn't supposed to be watching that looked very androgynous or even feminine. And that was an example of blurring the line between the solid black and white definitions of man and woman that God created.

The conversation ended with my mom hugging me. She reminded me that she loved me, and she just wanted me to be aware of what God wants for my life.

I couldn't wait for the lecture to be over for me to go to my room. I was tired and had a long day. I dropped my bags on the floor and fell onto my bed. I spent a few minutes just lying there. This last week was stressing me out so much. The Christmas Holiday was going to begin soon, but I was grounded, so I couldn't even enjoy that.

Finally, I rolled over and got out of bed. I dropped my uniform on the floor before stepping into my bathroom, and I turned on the shower. I relished the hot, steamy water for a while. It was such a relief after coming in from the bitter cold.

As I stood in the shower, I thought more of that day and the events that unfolded. *I was in love, wasn't I?* But not just with anyone. *With another boy?*

I shook my head. I knew that couldn't be the case. That was wrong, and I knew it. But I just couldn't shake these thoughts in my head. *Who was Ricky to me? Was he really just my friend?* Every second that I wasn't with him, I wished we were together. Or was it just that I was that lonely? I caught myself giving the wall a couple of punches. I was so frustrated and conflicted.

I stepped out of the shower and grabbed my towel to dry off as I stared at my reflection in the mirror. I told myself to ignore these thoughts. To forget all of this. Ricky was my friend, and that was it.

The rest of the school week went by without a hitch. I went to school, did my work, and returned home—nothing else. Friday was my trip to the library, but not this week. Not until my grounding was over.

Just like every year, we attended our church's Christmas Eve service, and that would be the last time I would see Ricky before school started again after New Year. It was getting old seeing my church. Five days a week for school. Then there was Sunday service. And then Christmas Eve, Good Friday, and so forth. But I enjoyed the Christmas Eve Service. It had a warm atmosphere.

The lights were dimmed, and the service was done entirely by candlelight. My younger siblings participated in the play that the Sunday School put on. Afterward, we read the nativity story in Luke, followed by a few Christmas carols. And then we were dismissed.

Another reason that I enjoyed this service was that it was the only one void of a lengthy sermon. Everything was wrapped up after about an hour. My mom and dad hung around visiting with some of the other church families. The kids hung out in the lobby or went downstairs to play. I quickly located Ricky, and we made our way to the lobby, where we threw on our jackets and slipped outside into the brisk winter air.

With our hands in our pockets, we made our way down the wooden steps and across the church parking lot. It wasn't too late. My watch read 7:00, but it was already pitch-black outside. And it had started snowing again.

As we continued walking, we could almost hear each snowflake as they landed softly on the snow-covered parking lot. I looked at Ricky, and I could see our breath hanging in the air. He smiled at me, and we came to a stop.

We were standing at the far edge of the church property, beside a wooden storage shed and a large mound of snow. We didn't have much chance to speak at school the last couple of days as we had been so busy preparing for the holiday. "How are you?" he asked. "My mom is worried about you. She didn't like the way Mr. Johnson was talking to us."

"I'm fine," I replied as I let out an audible sigh. "I'm used to it, anyway." I had this burning sensation welling up in my face. I quickly looked down and kicked a couple of pebbles with my foot.

"I wanted to ask you to come spend the night at my house during the holidays," he said. I looked up.

"I'm grounded, remember?"

"Your parents aren't going to relent, are they?"

"Not for a second," I said.

"Well, let's do that after school starts again," he suggested. That's what I loved about Ricky. He was always the optimist. But I knew my parents would never let me stay at his house. I've never been allowed to spend the night anywhere else but at my grandparents' house. Not since that summer at camp two years earlier.

There was a bench sitting off to the side. Usually this was a play area for the kids, but now there the huge snow mound that was pushed there by the snowplows who cleared the parking lot. When I was younger, I used to bring my crazy carpet from home and would slide down the hill with some of the other church kids. Now I felt I was too old for such childish behavior.

Brushing the snow away, we took a seat, and we both looked up at the starry sky. We sat there for a few moments without speaking. I had this familiar feeling. This time, as I looked up, I could identify *Taurus* and *Gemini*.

I was quick to point this out to Ricky, eager to have something to impress him with. He nodded. "You know, I've been reading a book about the constellations," he said.

"You are?" I asked with interest.

He nodded but didn't say anything more, and we sat there in silence for a few moments.

"You know, I'm going to miss not being able to see you," he said. "I will be doing things with my family, but I wish I could see you at the same time."

"I feel the same," I said. "It's okay. We can see each other after the holidays. But I'm not sure if I'll be allowed to sleep at your house."

He shrugged. "It's okay. No harm in trying, right?" I smiled and nodded, but I still had doubts.

There was a question that gnawed at me. I hesitated for a moment. I wasn't sure if I should ask it. I might not like the answer. Ricky looked at me and asked, "what's wrong?"

I blurted it out. "Do you... do you have a crush on anyone?"

He stared at me with a blank expression on his face for what seemed like an eternity. "Why do you ask?" he said.

"Oh, I don't know. Just curious, I guess." There was another moment of silence.

"There is someone," he said. I looked up.

"Who?" I asked.

He smiled at me. "It's a secret."

My heart sunk a little, but I tried to shrug it off. I was still conflicted about my feelings for him. Maybe it was just friendship and nothing more. What were the chances that he'd be into me in the same way, anyway? I smiled back, and we sat there in silence for a while longer, looking up at the night sky.

Our train of thought was interrupted by the sound of the church doors opening as a group of people made their way outside. I knew it was time to go. This would be our final goodbye until school resumed again two weeks later.

We both stood up, and I leaned into him. I'm not sure what I was expecting. But he moved towards me too and embraced me. I laid my head on his shoulder, and we stood there in silence. I felt his warm breath against my cheek. It was when I heard my sister calling my name that we broke apart. I looked him in the eye before joining my family. The drive home took forever. All I could think about was Ricky. The following two weeks already seemed like an eternity.

The next morning was Christmas. I usually was up early and full of excitement. But not today. I groggily sat up at the sound of the banging and commotion that was going on outside my bedroom.

My chest hurt. It felt like a hole was left there. I wasn't in the mood to do anything. I stayed in bed for as long as I could, but before long, I heard my dad knocking on my door. He stuck his head in my room and told me that breakfast was ready.

I glanced over at my alarm clock. It was half-past eight. I tossed the covers off with a little more gusto than I intended to and got myself ready for the day.

It was just after nine by the time I sat down at the table. I dressed in a pair of blue jeans and a T-shirt with a black hoodie. I was the only one fully dressed. All of my siblings were still in their pajamas, as well as my dad. My mom was in her bathrobe. She turned to me from where she was standing at the stove frying some bacon. "Aww, have you outgrown our traditions, honey?" she said to me with a smile.

Her cheerful voice irked me. I was still grounded, after all. I just mumbled an inaudible response as my dad started passing around plates of pancakes and sausages.

I can't lie. I still appreciated that Christmas was the one day where my parents cooked breakfast. Usually, we were on our own to prepare cereal or toast. But Christmas morning always meant pancakes, eggs, and sausages.

After we finished breakfast, we all sat around the tree for the gift opening. I received a new notebook, a couple of Christian movies, a devotional book, and a bunch of candy and chocolate. I wasn't feeling as enthusiastic as usual, but I still appreciated the gifts, and I let my parents know.

After our gift opening was done, we quickly cleaned up and got ready to go to our grandma and grandpa's house. Or Oma and Opa, as we called them in Dutch. It was a tradition to go to their house every Christmas. We went shortly after opening our gifts and would spend the night.

It was always a great time, and we looked forward to it. But this year I wasn't as enthusiastic as in previous years. It could have been that I was just getting older, but I was also preoccupied with my thoughts. I missed Ricky and wanted nothing more than to see him again.

After greeting both of my grandparents and my aunt and uncle, who already arrived, I helped myself to a couple of shortbread cookies, pulled out the Japanese book I was studying, and found a corner on the sofa where I could read in peace.

After a few moments, I laid the book down. I couldn't concentrate, and so I rested my head on the armrest. When I opened my eyes again, I was surprised at what stood before me.

It was Ricky. He was leaning over me and smiling from ear to ear. I shook my head as I sat up. Was I dreaming? "What are you doing here?" I asked with surprise. He placed his warm hand over mine. Then leaned his face in towards mine. He whispered in my ear, "I miss you."

"I miss you too," I said back. His eyes were so gorgeous. They were one of my favorite attributes of his.

"Merry Christmas," he said. He kept smiling. "I brought you a gift," and with that, his lips met mine. I accepted willingly, and my mouth opened to receive his. I closed my eyes and used my other senses to savor this moment. I could smell him. I could taste his breath. It aroused me.

When he pulled back, it was too soon and left me wanting more. I opened my eyes to see my cousin, Peter, standing in front of me. I jumped back.

He was the same age as me, but a little shorter and stouter. He sported a head of bright red hair. That came from the Irish on his dad's side. His mom was my mom's sister.

"Hey," I said as I gave my head a shake. I looked around. Ricky was gone.

"We're going for a sleigh ride. Do you want to come with us?"

My opa must have had the team of horses out. Going for a

sleigh ride was one of my favorite things to do on the farm. I sat up and brushed the sleep out of my eyes.

"Yea, sure," I said.

It was like the famous song, *Jingle Bells*. Waist-high snow covering the fields for as far as the eye could see. My opa's team of horses vigorously crashed through the snow, with the bells hanging from their harness being audible for miles around.

We sat on square hay bales, and I had a scarf wrapped tightly around my face as well as my hood pulled up over my head. I enjoyed our annual Christmas sleigh ride, but it still didn't change my feelings about winter and the cold that came with it. The only thing that would make this better was if Ricky could sit beside me and enjoy this moment with me. If I closed my eyes and concentrated hard enough, I could almost sense him sitting beside me.

The hot chocolate was a welcome sight when we made it back inside the house. I quickly slipped out of my wet clothes and took a hot shower before helping myself to a steaming mug. I topped it off with a generous helping of whipped cream and candy sprinkles.

I then sat on the sofa with Peter. He received a Game Boy Advanced as well as the new Pokémon Emerald game. My parents wouldn't let me have a Game Boy. I asked many times, but they considered it a waste of time and money. On top of that, most of the games that I would want to play were deemed to be evil. Pokémon was the tamest of them, but our school had a Bible Study lesson recently where we were told that Pokémon were named after demons. My mom also told me it was occultic. I read a book from the library about the occult, and I quickly learned that my mom had no idea what the occult actually was. But it wasn't worth arguing about.

When I was with my relatives, my mom realized her beliefs sounded ridiculous. So, she didn't say anything as I played with my cousin. It was my one time of freedom. Otherwise, I always hid my books or movies under my bed.

We finished the day with a scrumptious Christmas Dinner. All three of my mom's sisters were there with their families. I had five cousins in total. Peter and I were both the oldest, and usually, we hung out together, just the two of us.

We did our gift exchange. This was the highlight for the kids, but as I got older, it was less exciting. I still enjoyed getting more sweets, and my Oma always slipped me some money. Fifty dollars this year. Usually, I used it to buy more anime DVDs, but I recently decided that I was going to take a trip to Japan. I decided to put this money aside for that.

As I was watching my younger siblings and cousins tear their presents open, I overheard my mom and my Aunt Sarah talking in hushed whispers. My mom was at odds with her family over many issues. My parents were very conservative, but my mom's sisters and parents weren't. At least not to the same degree.

I had no idea how my mom drifted so much from her family, but I assumed it happened after meeting my dad. I barely saw my grandparents on his side, as they lived quite far away. My dad also didn't have any siblings, so it was just his parents. Typically, we'd make a trip to see them closer to New Year's. But I never enjoyed going to their house as much. Part of it was the lack of cousins to hang out with. They were also very conservative. Even more so than my parents.

We couldn't visit them without dressing up in nice clothes. A Bible Reading prefaced every meal, and the King James Version was the only acceptable Bible. I got enough of that at home and school, and it was a point of contention that it followed me to my grandparents' place too. I was forbidden from bringing any of my books or games, as they were just as critical as my parents were.

The last time I was there, I brought a Japanese Study book from the library, and I got an earful from my grandma. She told me that America was the absolute best country in the world. There was no point in getting interested in another country as nowhere could compare to our great country. Even learning a foreign language was pointless as most of the world should speak English, anyway. So, I learned the hard way that I couldn't bring anything except a Bible and my Sunday best.

But my mom's side was more laid back. My Aunt Sarah was probably the most open-minded of them, and she was by far my favorite aunt. She often got into minor spats with my mom. Nothing was ever too serious, but this time, I overheard them talking about our schooling.

My aunt had been doing some research and found out that the school we went to was associated with a cult group from Texas. The leader of the group was accused by a student for having made inappropriate comments towards her at one of the big annual student conventions. The allegations went as far as accusing him of trying to make a move on her. The organization's leadership did their best to shove this under the rug.

My mom just scoffed. "Reverend Howard is the godliest man in all of America. And by the grace of God, he has developed a school curriculum that places God at the center of our children's education."

Out of the corner of my eye, I saw my aunt give a dramatic eye roll. I then quickly looked straight ahead. I didn't want them to notice that I was eavesdropping.

"The guy's a cult leader," my aunt replied with incredulity in her voice. "It's been clearly documented. And if you look at his private life, he's a hypocrite. Not only are some of his ideas harmful, but by sending your kids to that school, you're just lining his pockets."

I secretly wanted to give my aunt a high five. She was saying things I was already aware of due to having done my research on the library's computers. It was reassuring to know that she was on my side.

I listened to them for a few more minutes. My mom wouldn't budge from her stance. I knew she wouldn't. But I still loved to see my aunt push back on her beliefs from time to time. "There's also the fact that the curriculum isn't accredited with the government," my aunt pointed out.

"We don't need this secular government to decide what is and isn't a good education system. They kicked God out of school a long time ago. So, how can they be trusted?"

My aunt continued, "well, for starters, it's going to be harder for the kids to get into university if they don't have a diploma."

"Maybe not going to university is what's best for them," my mom replied. "They've been hijacked by liberal professors who are filling our kids' heads with garbage. Like gender studies and such."

The argument went on for a while. One of my mom's attributes was that she was stubborn in her beliefs. There would be no swaying her.

What made me anxious was that my aunt was correct. And it crossed my mind often that when I graduated, it would be tough for me to attend university. I wouldn't have a diploma. I could check with the public school to see if it was possible to challenge the exams, but that was something that worried me for now.

That night Peter and I slept side by side on our oma's living room floor. A couple of my siblings, as well as Peter's younger sister, were nearby, too.

Our parents were in the two guest rooms. Peter and I stayed up late playing the Game Boy. That lasted until Oma came out and hollered at us to go to sleep. I guess we were making more noise than we realized.

It was about an hour later when I woke up. My bladder was calling. I stood up and slowly tip-toed around the sleeping bodies. I found the hallway light and flipped it on as I made my way to the bathroom.

It was when I stood over the toilet that I sensed something beside me: something or someone. I looked out of the corner of my eye.

It was Ricky. He was standing there with a smile on his face. I stood there wide-eyed with disbelief. I quickly finished my business, but when I turned back to him, he was gone. I was standing alone in the bathroom. I checked behind the shower curtains. Then poked my head out the bathroom door. Nothing. I was positive he had been there with me.

It was on the way back that I realized the hallway was darker than I thought it was. Even with the light on, it gave me the creeps. I sensed movement in every shadow as I slowly made my way through the hallway. It occurred to me just how long the hallway was.

On reaching the end, I quickly ran and jumped under my covers. I looked around and saw that everyone was still sleeping. It was then that I let out a huge sigh, followed by a sob. I kept the covers over my head to muffle the sound of my crying.

My parents were too strict. We went to a school that used corporal punishment and public humiliation for discipline. I had to hide any movies or books that I enjoyed. I was forced to read the King James Bible. I would never be able to go to university.

And most of all, I missed Ricky. It would be another week before school began, and that seemed like an eternity. I closed my eyes, hoping that when I opened them again, I would be free from this nightmare.

CHAPTER 5

I jumped awake at the sound of my alarm clock. I never got out of bed so quickly before. Especially not on a school day.

I took a much shorter shower than was the norm, and I used a generous amount of cologne after I put on my uniform. I got my dad to help with my tie. Often I struggled and would eventually do it myself, but this time I wanted it to look perfect.

It was the first week of January, and it was still cold outside, but even that couldn't get my spirits down. I practically ran up the steps and into the church building. Ricky hadn't arrived yet, so I set my backpack at my desk, and I got out the books that I took home for the Christmas Holiday. Today my grounding ended too. One more thing worth celebrating.

By the time we started the morning pledges and Bible reading, Ricky still hadn't arrived. My heart was pounding in my chest with anticipation.

By lunchtime, Ricky still wasn't at school, so I finally asked Mr. Johnson. It was then I learned that Ricky's parents had pulled him from the school. He wouldn't be returning. My heart fell, and my words caught in my throat. I couldn't reply. I just turned around and made my way to the bathroom.

The instant I entered the room, the tears streamed down my cheeks. I couldn't help myself. "What's the matter with you?" came a voice. It was one of the older boys.

"Nothing," I muttered, and I locked myself in one cubicle. I trembled uncontrollably at this point. I couldn't believe what I heard. Where was Ricky? How could he just stop and not even tell me?

I stayed in there longer than I meant to. But I had no motivation to do anything. I was so confused and upset. Was Ricky mad at me about something? Did he get weirded out because he realized that I was developing a crush on him? I had so many questions, but he wasn't here to answer them.

Realizing I was going to be missed if I didn't return to class, I unlocked the cubicle and walked to the sink, where I did my best to wash my face. I stared at my reflection. My eyes were puffy, and my face was still quite red. I hoped no one would notice.

I returned to my table, where I sat stock still, staring at my food without taking a bite. I was numb. I couldn't put into words how I was feeling.

The rest of the school day dragged on forever. I couldn't wait to get home. I didn't have any motivation to study, nor did I have the concentration to do anything. I spent most of my day idly staring at my work packs. I ended up taking most of it home as homework. But I didn't care. I couldn't wait to leave. I wanted to be alone.

During the ride home, my mom tried to talk to me. She asked how my first day back was. I evaded the questions. I didn't want to think about it, but she noticed.

"Jeremiah, what's the matter?" she asked.

"I don't want to talk about it," I said.

My mom had an expression of concern on her face, and she persisted. "What's wrong? Did something happen at school?"

As much as I didn't want to talk about it, I couldn't help it, and I blurted it out. "Ricky dropped out of school."

"Oh? That's weird. I wonder if something happened."

"I don't know," I said as I stared out the window at the passing fields. I felt like crying. I couldn't remember the last time that I felt that miserable and depressed.

"Don't stress about it too much," my mom said. "We'll see him at church. I'm sure you can talk to him then and find out what happened."

"Maybe," I said, not in the mood to engage with this line of questioning.

When we got home, I made a beeline for the house, ignoring my mom calling me to help bring the groceries inside.

"Hey," my dad said to me as I walked past him into the living room. "How was school?"

I didn't reply. I slammed my bedroom door shut, and I jumped onto my bed, where I sobbed into my pillow.

I'm not sure how long I had been lying there. I must have fallen asleep, because a soft tapping on my door woke me up. My face was wet, and I wiped it with the sleeve of my shirt. "Come in," I said meekly, and my dad stuck his head in my room.

"Hey, everything alright?" he asked. I nodded. Maybe he wouldn't see my wet face in the darkness. "Don't lie," he said to me as he came into my room and took a seat on my bed. "Your mom told me."

"Oh," I I pushed myself into a sitting position. I took a deep breath before I tried to speak again. "Do you think I'm being immature about this?"

"Not at all," my dad said. "I lost a good friend once too."

"What happened?" My curiosity got the better of me.

"I was about your age," my dad said to me as he recalled memories from long ago. "He was my best friend at school. We were always together. People used to joke that we were brothers. I was always at his house, or he was always at mine. Then one day, he just stopped talking to me."

"Really? What happened?"

My dad let out a sigh. "He met a girl. And then decided that he didn't have room for friends. His entire life revolved around this girl. And so, he ignored me. After we finished high school, I never saw him again."

"Are you telling me that story to make me feel better?" I asked. "Because it didn't."

"I just wanted you to know that these things happen sometimes. You're not alone," he replied.

"Well, what should I do?" I asked him.

"As your mom said, you can wait for Sunday and talk to him at church. See what's going on. I'm sure that it's nothing personal."

"I can't wait that long," I protested. "I'm going crazy trying to think of what could have possibly happened."

"As I said, I'm sure it's nothing," my dad tried to reassure me.

I thought for a moment. "Would it be okay if I phoned him?"

There was a moment of silence before my dad answered. "I think that might be a good idea. But you'd better hurry. We're about to eat."

I dashed to the bathroom, where I wiped my face and changed my clothes. I then went to the kitchen and found the phone directory. I flipped through the pages.

"What are you doing?" my mom asked as she set the table.

"Dad said that it was okay to call Ricky," I said. "I just want to make sure that everything's alright."

I ran my finger down the list of last names that began with the letter V. I searched for a minute, and then I found it. I took the phone off the wall and dialed the number. After a moment, there was an answer on the other end. "Hello, Vergara residence."

"Hello, Mrs. Vergara? This is Jeremiah."

"Oh hi. How are you?"

"I'm fine, thanks." My chest was getting tight. "Is Ricky there?" I asked.

"Yes, sure. Just wait a minute. I'll put him on."

The thirty seconds that I waited seemed like an eternity. I didn't even know what to say. But I had to come up with something fast. Ricky's voice came from the other end of the receiver. "Hello?"

"Hi. It's me, Jeremiah." Feeling the anxiety building up, I waited for his reply.

"Oh, hi." There was an awkward pause on his end. "What's up?" he asked.

"You dropped out of school?" Maybe it was stupid, but that was the first thing that came to mind.

There was a moment of silence before he answered. "I'm sorry. I was going to call and tell you."

I processed that for a moment. Then I asked, "What happened?"

"My parents aren't happy with the school. Especially my mom. After your punishment in front of everyone. And then us getting called in because we were sitting together. She said that was the most ridiculous thing that she'd ever heard of. And so, I'm going to the public school now."

"I'm going to miss you," I said, hoping that didn't sound too corny. I was still trying to get over what was happening.

"I'll miss you too," he replied. "You're what will be the hardest to leave. I'll miss our lunchtime chats."

I felt my voice quivering. "Will I see you again?"

His voice was calm and reassuring. "We'll still be going to the church. I'll see you on Sundays."

"Okay," I said. "That's something."

"Actually, would you like to come sleep at my house next weekend?"

"Really? I'd love to." Then I glanced over at my mom, who was busy stirring a large pot of stew. "But I've never gone on a sleepover before. I don't think my mom would let me."

"Let my mom talk to her," Ricky replied. "We'll discuss a date, and then my mom can talk to yours on Sunday. How does that sound?"

"Okay, it's worth a shot," I replied.

The rest of the school week dragged on. Sunday just couldn't come fast enough. I didn't get to talk to Ricky until then, but seeing him at church kept me going.

By the time Sunday arrived, I was pumped. Upon laying my eyes on Ricky, it took all of my willpower not to jump at him and embrace him. Instead, I smiled when our eyes met.

That day's service took longer than expected. Our pastor often liked to bring up things he came across in the news. This time it was from the international section.

There were reports that Canada was planning to legalize same-sex marriage. Our pastor made it clear what his stance was on that matter. We sat through a thirty-minute lecture on why homosexuality was wrong. How all gays were going to go to hell for this sin, which was one of the worst things you could do.

I was at a point in my life where I was confused and struggling with my feelings. On the one hand, I was attracted to Ricky. But I had to keep bringing myself back to reality. I wasn't gay. I couldn't be. I knew it was wrong and went against God's will.

But the more I listened to the sermon, the more I thought to myself, *Why was it wrong*? I mean, think about it. What is wrong with two boys or two girls being in a relationship with each other? Unlike murder or theft, being gay didn't hurt anyone else.

I was never that attentive during a sermon before, but it wasn't out of interest this time. It left a bitter taste in my mouth, and I was filled with a mix of emotions.

When it ended, I couldn't be more relieved. I couldn't stomach any more of that. I immediately got up and made my way to Ricky. He was dressed more formally than usual. This time he was wearing an attractive gray suit jacket with a red necktie and navy blue pants. Maybe I was gay after all. I found myself attracted to him even more than before. I also noticed that his hair was combed to one side. I liked that.

"How are you?" he asked. I stumbled for words as I was distracted, sizing him up. I could feel my cheeks get hot.

"I'm okay," I replied. "It's been a long time."

"I know," he said. "Did you have a good Christmas?"

"Yea, it was fine," I said. That was a lie. It hadn't been a bad Christmas, but I spent most of it longing for this moment.

"Oh, hey Jeremiah, it's so nice to see you again," said Ricky's mom as she finished speaking with a couple of church ladies and turned towards us.

"Hi Mrs. Vergara," I said. "It's nice to see you again."

"Is your mother around?" she asked.

I nodded and pointed to where my mom was standing, chatting with a bunch of other ladies.

"Ok, that's great. I wanted to talk with her," and off she went down the row of pews.

"What do you think she'll say?" Ricky asked me.

I shrugged. "She'll probably say no."

"I hope not," Ricky said. I just couldn't get over how cute he was, and I stared at his dimples.

We sat down on an empty pew while we waited for our

mothers to finish talking. "So, if my mom lets me sleep at your house, did you have anything planned?" I asked.

He thought for a moment. "I wanted to go to a movie."

"Really?" I tried to contain my excitement. I had never been to a movie before. But then I had a sinking feeling, and I shook my head. "My mom would never let me go. She hates movies. She thinks Hollywood is trying to destroy society."

Ricky smirked for a moment. Then the look on his face told me he realized I was serious. "You mean you've never been before?"

"Never," I said. "I watch some anime at home. And my mom lets us watch family movies sometimes too. But that's it."

"It's okay," Ricky said. "We don't need to tell them. My mom will take us, so it'll be fine."

"Yea, if I'm allowed to go at all," I said as I glanced over at my mom and Mrs. Vergara. They were still talking. I was nervous to know the outcome. But going for a sleepover at Ricky's house would be amazing.

I still didn't know the outcome of the conversation during the ride home. I sat in the middle seat, right behind my dad, who was driving. My mom was in the passenger seat beside him.

My mom turned around to look at me. "So, I was talking to Ricky's mom."

"Okay," I said, anxious to know the answer.

"Ricky wants you to go to his house for a sleepover."

"Okay," I said again. I couldn't take the suspense.

"Your father and I will talk about it more at home."

"Okay," I said for the third time. "So, you're not saying no?"

"We will think about it," she replied.

"You know that I've never been to a sleepover before," I said. "I really want to. It will be lots of fun."

"I'm sure it would be," my mom said. "And the Vergara's are nice people and active members of the church. So that makes us feel more comfortable about letting you go."

I couldn't contain myself. Was she saying that I could go?

"So, your father and I will talk about it at home. You are fourteen now, so maybe time to give you a little more freedom."

I sat back and tried to relax for the rest of the ride home. I was happy to hear my mom say that, and I hoped they would let me go.

In the end, they did let me sleep at his house. But they had a list of conditions that the Vergaras had to agree to first. They weren't to allow me to have access to any secular movies or books. That included going to the cinema.

They also didn't want me to go to the city. Mrs. Vergara suggested going to the mall for a day, but my parents both put their foot down on that. They said that it provided too many temptations.

Finally, I had to do well at school during the upcoming week first and have no homework that needed to be done. If I did, then I couldn't go.

My parents told me it would be a trial run. If everything went without a problem, then they may allow me to go more often.

I was disappointed at how strict they were going to be with the rules. But at least I could go. That was still something, and so I gave an enthusiastic *yes* to their stipulations. As fortune would have, Mrs. Vergara somehow got them to agree to two nights. I would go on Friday after school and then go back home on Sunday after church. I couldn't contain myself; I was so excited.

The following week dragged on forever. I constantly thought about Friday. Despite that, I made sure to not get too distracted, as I had to get all of my work done for the week.

I woke up earlier than usual on Friday morning and quickly packed my bag. The minutes dragged by at a snail's pace.

When the final school bell rang, I rushed to collect my things. I ran outside, and I saw his face smiling at me from under his hood. It was getting chilly outside, so I pulled my hood over my head as I walked up to meet him. His mother was sitting inside the car waiting for us.

He lived in town, so it was only a two-minute drive to his house. He lived in a lovely middle-class suburban home with his parents. His mom worked as a food caterer, while his dad worked in a warehouse. His older sister, Claire, and her twin sister, Angel, were there as well. They were eighteen and worked with their mom.

His dad and sisters greeted me warmly and helped me bring my bags in from the car. I would share a room with Ricky. It was my first time sharing a bedroom with someone that wasn't family.

He had a double bed with bedding sporting images from *Dragon Ball Z*, one of our favorite TV shows. We set my bags at the foot of his bed.

"You can sleep in my bed," he said with a smile. "I'll sleep on the floor. I have more bedding."

"Are you sure?" I asked. I felt a pang of guilt that he had to sleep on the floor in his own bedroom.

"We could both sleep in my bed if you want," he said. I glanced down at my feet. My cheeks were probably bright crimson by now.

"It's ok," he said. "I'll sleep on the floor. It's completely fine."

I wanted to share a bed with him. But I didn't know how to say that without things getting awkward between us. I didn't want to suggest anything that seemed gay. What would he think of me? Besides, he had a crush on someone, so it's not like he was interested in me, anyway.

I took off my winter jacket. My school uniform was soaked with sweat. "Can I use your bathroom?" I asked him. This wasn't my first time at his house. I had spent many afternoons here, but I still felt a little shy.

"Yea, of course," he replied. I grabbed my backpack and made my way down the hallway to the bathroom.

I changed out of my uniform and put on a T-shirt, blue jeans, and a red hoodie. I stared at my reflection in the mirror. For the first time in a while, I sized myself up.

My right ear looked a little bigger than the left one. I had a couple of freckles under my eye that I hadn't noticed before. My front tooth seemed crooked. I was skinny, and some of the kids poked fun at me about that from time to time.

I took a deep breath as I stared at my reflection. I felt very self-conscious of my looks. I pulled out a bottle of cologne from my backpack and gave myself a couple of sprays.

I was still conflicted. Ricky and I were just good friends. He was my best friend. But that was it. So why did I have this urge to impress him? If he was really my friend, then he would like me regardless of how I looked.

Stuffing my things back into my bag, I made my way back to his bedroom. He sat at the edge of his bed as he pulled a change of clothes out of his dresser. He was completely nude except for a pair of blue underwear. I immediately diverted my eyes.

"I'm sorry," I said. "I didn't know that you were changing."

"Your family really does shelter you, don't they?" he said. "We're both boys. There's nothing to hide."

"Yea, you're right," I replied. But I still kept my eyes down. It reminded me of the kids back at camp. It baffled me how comfortable they were changing in front of each other. I still hadn't gotten over my shyness. I was a little curious, and it occurred to me to take a glance at him, but my awkwardness got the better of me, and I sat at the other end of the bed, facing away from my friend as I set my bag down.

"So, what did you want to do this weekend?" Ricky asked.

"I'm up for anything. What did you have in mind?" I asked without looking at him.

"Well," he said as he let out an audible sigh. "Your mom gave my mom an extensive list of things that we can't do."

"Yea, she did," I acknowledged. "Sorry about that."

"What's there to be sorry about?" he asked, and I sensed movement. I looked up to see him sitting beside me. He was dressed in a pair of bright orange basketball shorts and a T-shirt. He must have forgotten that it was -30° outside. "It's not your fault that your mom is so strict," he said. "But we'll have a good weekend. I promise."

For dinner, his mom made my favorite Filipino dish, pork adobo. Eating at their house was always a welcome break from our daily fare of potatoes and stew. My mom was a good cook, but it got boring after a while. I enjoyed the change.

After dinner, we showered and then sat in the living room to watch a movie. I brought a pair of pajamas. Ricky was just wearing a pair of shorts and a muscle shirt. His parents went to bed before us. They asked us to keep the volume low, and not to stay up too late.

"I know your mom said that we weren't allowed," Ricky said, "but my mom said that it's fine. As long as we don't say anything."

He then inserted a DVD into the DVD player. "We went to the city last weekend, and I bought this Box Set." It was for an anime show called *Witch Hunter Robin*.

I hadn't seen it before, but I heard about it. My mom definitely wouldn't have approved of it. It was about a girl who came to Japan to help an organization hunt down and deal with witches who were wreaking havoc. But the catch was that the girl was a witch herself and had to learn how to harness her powers.

Witches. Dark magic. Occult imagery. All the things my mom would be horrified to know that I was into. But it was fantasy. Just make-believe. I never could understand why it bothered her so much.

This was the first time that I could watch something like this in the open. Usually, I recorded shows on TV and waited for my mom to go to work before I watched them.

Ricky and I both took a seat on the sofa with a bowl of popcorn that Mrs. Vergara prepared for us. After about an hour, we were both yawning. Not able to keep our eyes open anymore, we decided to watch more of the show the next day.

Back in his room, I crept into his bed while he took his place on the floor. It took everything to resist the urge to ask him to join me in the bed. That was a bit too far. So, I didn't say anything as he laid out bedding on the floor.

It often took me longer to fall asleep when I was away from home, but I was exhausted tonight. I laid over on my stomach with my arm dangling off the bed, and I shut my eyes. I felt sleep creeping up on me.

I almost swore I felt a hand brush up against mine. It happened once. And then again. On the third time, I felt fingers slowly intertwine with mine, and it gave me a sense of security.

I closed my eyes and took a deep breath, and then everything went dark.

CHAPTER 6

Despite it being a weekend, I was up at 6:00 AM. Even at my house, I couldn't sleep in, but especially when I slept away from home. I glanced down and saw Ricky sleeping peacefully. His soft breathing was soothing, so I laid back down and relaxed.

After about thirty minutes, I sat up and slipped on a pair of jeans before making my way to the bathroom to relieve myself. As I stealthily walked back to the bedroom, I heard someone moving around in the kitchen. I took a slight detour and stuck my head around the corner. Mrs. Vergara was standing over the stove frying eggs. She looked at me and smiled.

"Did you sleep well, honey?" she asked me. I blushed. She was the only one other than my mom who called me that.

"Yes, thank you," I replied. "Ricky's still sleeping. I've been up for a little while."

"Oh, don't mind him," she said as she scooped up the fried eggs and put them on a serving plate. "It's Saturday. He'll sleep until noon if I let him."

I didn't know what else to say, and I took a seat at the kitchen table. "Mr. Vergara will be up soon, so I have a pot of coffee on. Do you drink coffee?"

"Yes please," I replied. My dad was a big coffee drinker, and I recently started drinking it with him.

"Do you take anything in it?" she asked as she put a cover on the eggs. And then grabbed a couple of coffee mugs.

"No, just black is fine," I said. Both my dad and grandma drank black coffee. I used to take mine with milk in it, but they teased me, telling me I'll never grow up to be a man that way. So, I learned to drink it black. Now I couldn't imagine putting anything in it.

Mrs. Vergara passed me a cup of coffee, and she took a seat

across from me with a cup of her own. "So, how would you like to go to the mall today?"

"Really? I'd love that. But... my mom won't let me."

Mrs. Vergara smiled at me. "I know, but it's okay. If you want to go, then we will. Just don't tell her. Ricky wants to take you."

I couldn't believe my luck. "That would be awesome. Are you sure? You aren't worried you'll get into trouble with my parents?"

"No, it's okay," she said. "I want you guys to go and have a great time. And Ricky told me that you often don't get to do things like that."

"That's true," I nodded.

"Jeremiah, do you know why we pulled Ricky out of your school?" she asked me.

"No, I don't," I replied. Ricky had told me they weren't happy about the way I was treated when I got caught for cheating, but he never explained in detail what made them pull him out.

"We didn't want to," she said. "He's made a great friend in you. And he wasn't pleased when we told him the news. But there were some problems that we've had with the school. Here, let me explain." She looked off to the side for a moment or two. She seemed to be deciding how to word what she was about to say.

"When we came here from the Philippines, one of the first things we wanted to do was to find a local church to attend," she told me. "And a lady who helped us to get settled here suggested the church that we're attending now. She told me that the school is excellent as well. I liked the idea of giving Ricky a Christian education, so we sent him there." She took a sip of her coffee. I realized that mine was getting cold too, so I brought the cup to my lips.

Mrs. Vergara continued, "We were happy with the school in the beginning, and all of the staff seemed very nice and friendly. But after a couple of months, I started taking a closer look at Ricky's schoolwork, and I became concerned with some of the material that he was being taught."

She took another sip of her coffee before she continued. "And there were other incidents. I found out from another lady at church that the school doesn't even hire licensed teachers. They're all parents who volunteer. And then there were the punishments. I heard about kids getting locked in cupboards, and you getting paddled like that in public. That was awful. Then I didn't appreciate when Mr. Johnson called me in and was accusing you boys of being what exactly? Friends?"

She shook her head, and I could see that she was getting upset. She brushed away a tear. "So, I decided to put Ricky in the public school. It's only been a week now, but he seems to be enjoying it and doing much better."

I didn't know how I should respond, so I just looked down at the table and took another sip of coffee.

"Anyway, never mind that," she said. "I just wanted you to know that it had nothing to do with you. And I do feel sorry that you're still stuck there."

I looked up at her. I knew she was right about the school, and it hurt. It really was that awful there, but my mom wouldn't even consider other options. Ricky was the only thing at the school that I had going for me, and even that had now been taken away.

"Oh, sorry," she said. "I hope that I'm not overstepping. Ricky told me how strict your parents are and how stressful it has been on you."

I didn't do anything but nod. She continued. "You need room to explore new things. So, I thought it would be nice to take you boys on a trip to the city. You need room to explore new things. I know you'll have a great time. Just don't tell your mom, okay?" She gave me a wink and then got up and went back to the stove to finish what she had been doing. It occurred to me that I loved Mrs. Vergara more than ever. I was jealous of how cool Ricky's family was. Today was going to be a great day.

Mrs. Vergara practically dragged Ricky out of bed thirty minutes later. He took a shower and joined us at the table. There was still sleep in his eyes.

Mrs. Vergara was an excellent cook. This wasn't the first time that I ate at their house, but I'd never had breakfast there.

Whenever I've been at their house, Mrs. Vergara always made traditional Filipino dishes. This time, she cooked a Western-style breakfast, but it was still excellent. Fried eggs, breakfast sausages, bacon, and hash browns.

After we ate, I took a shower, and we got ready to go to the city, which was a two-hour car drive away. The plan was to go to the shopping mall where we'd go to the water park, do some shopping, watch a movie, and then have dinner before coming back home.

My parents had taken me to the mall occasionally, but the cinema was off-limits. The water park was as well. My mom thought I'd get dirty thoughts in my head from seeing so many scantily clad girls. She didn't approve of two-piece bathing suits. My sisters had to wear these ugly one-piece suits that practically covered them from head to toe, like something that women used to wear in the 1940s. The only time we were allowed to go swimming was at the local pool in our town. It was primarily families from our church who went there, so my parents weren't worried about what others might be wearing. They all had the same view regarding that.

Although I owned a pair of swimming trunks, I didn't think to bring them. Ricky let me borrow a pair of his. He was a little shorter than me, but they fit fine enough.

Ricky's dad came with us as well, while his sisters stayed home. They were going out with their friend.

Ricky's parents went to meet with some friends while the two of us headed straight to the water park. It was a massive facility and was one of the biggest attractions at the mall.

It was in the changing room that I had anxiety. I still couldn't get over the fact that everyone was comfortable changing out in the open. It was like being back at camp.

Ricky and I both shared a locker. I took the trunks out of the bag and then stood there awkwardly as Ricky took off his shirt. "What's wrong?" he asked.

"Are there stalls that I could use to change in?" I asked. He gave me a questioning look as he unbuttoned his jeans.

"Yea, over there. But what's the matter? It's just us guys here." He then pulled down his jeans and underwear and turned around to pick up his trunks that were sitting on a nearby bench. I couldn't help but lay my eyes on his beautifully tanned skin. And I noticed how smooth and round his buttocks were as well.

He stepped out of his pants and straightened himself with his trunks in his hand. I quickly diverted my eyes. I could feel my cheeks burning.

"I'll be back," I mumbled, and I made my way to the cubicles as fast as my feet would take me. I had a tight, uncomfortable feeling in my pants, and I was terrified that someone might notice.

After changing into the trunks, I waited for a few more minutes to make sure I calmed down completely and didn't leave any telltale signs of arousal.

I couldn't get over how massive this facility was. It was nothing like the small-town swimming pool that I was used to.

The first thing that I noticed was the very humid air. I never traveled abroad before, but this is how I imagined the beach in a far-off tropical country would feel.

There was a giant wave pool. It was at least twenty times as large as my home pool. And at the edge, the concrete was a sandy brown color, as if to help recreate the feeling of being on a balmy beach.

There were so many slides that I couldn't decide which one to go on first. Ricky grabbed me by the hand and led the way up the stairs. We started on one called *The Twister*. The top of the slide was probably as high as a six-story building. I was anxious and excited at the same time. I let Ricky go first, and I went shortly after him.

I slid down and immediately entered a dark tunnel. I couldn't see a thing, but could feel myself speeding around the many bends and turns as water splashed me in the face. The entire trip took about thirty seconds before I landed in a shallow pool. I came out gasping for air and looked to see Ricky sitting at the edge of the pool, smiling at me.

We then spent the next four hours going from slide to slide and even went for a swim together in the wave pool. Seeing as it was Saturday, it was packed with families, and some of the slides had a long waiting time, but it was still a wonderful day.

When we finally had enough, we changed into our clothes and met Ricky's parents, who took us to the food court for lunch. Fast food was a rare treat for me.

We had an hour before the movie started, so we went to a couple of clothing stores. Much to my surprise, Mrs. Vergara offered to buy me something. Ricky and I both got matching hoodies displaying one of our favorite anime shows.

Once it was time for the movie to start, Ricky's parents went on their own to go shopping after giving us money for the cinema. We both got our own soft drink and a large bag of popcorn to share.

Ricky wanted to see a new horror movie that had recently come out. I wasn't particularly interested in horror movies, but it was about a haunting in Japan, and so I agreed to check it out, purely because of my blooming interest in Japanese culture.

The cinema wasn't as full as we expected it to be, and we found a spot in the back to sit. The movie turned out to be quite interesting, with only some mild scares.

We were about halfway through when I felt something nudge my hand. I looked over at Ricky. I couldn't make out his face in the dark, but he was staring straight ahead at the screen, so I resumed watching the movie. And then it happened again. This time, I felt his hand wrap around mine. His hand was warm, and I liked that feeling.

He held my hand like that for a few moments and then intertwined his fingers with mine. My heart was beating furiously in my chest at this point, and I couldn't concentrate on the movie. I gave a side glance in his direction, but he was still staring ahead at the screen. I leaned back in my seat and tried to concentrate on the movie. I was getting a funny sensation in my stomach. Like I had butterflies. Is this what it felt like to have a crush on someone? Wait, not a crush. He was a boy. I didn't have a crush on another boy. But what did I feel about him? Why was this making me feel so funny on the inside?

A part of me was relieved when the movie finally ended, and

our hands broke apart, but another part of me felt disappointed as well. Why was I still so conflicted about this?

The drive home was quiet and uneventful. Ricky's mom asked us many questions about our time at the cinema and the water park. I tried to make conversation with Ricky but wasn't sure what to say. We were together the entire day, after all.

Before long, he was asleep, and his head rested on my shoulder. We were both exhausted from a long but fun day, and soon I followed him into dreamland. My last thoughts were that I was sad it was my last night with Ricky and his family, and I hoped my parents would allow me to come back another time.

As I lay in bed contemplating this, I rolled over and looked at Ricky, who was comfortable on the floor. He looked up at me.

"Thanks for inviting me," I said. "I had a lot of fun with you."

"I had a lot of fun, too," he replied. There was a moment of silence between us.

"I'm sorry that I dropped out of school," he continued. "But we'll still see each other at church, and hopefully, you can come sleep here again soon."

I smiled. "I would like that," I said. And then I thought of something. "You don't need to sleep on the floor, you know. I mean, this is your room after all."

He gave me a questioning glance and said, "What do you mean?"

It was a good thing that it was dark because my face was probably as red as a tomato. "I mean, would you like to sleep in your bed as well? With me I mean."

I wished I hadn't said that the instant the words left my mouth. I quickly put my head under the covers as I nervously awaited his response. *Ugh, you idiot,* I thought. *He's going to say no, and now he thinks you're weird. And he'll never invite you to come back here again.*

His response was not at all what I expected. "Sure," he said.

"Really?" I said in disbelief, and I scooted over to give him room as he climbed in beside me. We laid there for a moment, staring at each other. I could barely make out his face, yet I could still see his beautiful eyes staring at me.

As surprised as I was that he took me up on my offer, what happened next was even more unexpected. He brought his face towards mine. Our lips met, and I felt his tongue enter my mouth. My tongue met his as they wrestled with each other for a minute before we broke apart.

He kissed me? I thought to myself. *Did he really just kiss me?* I gave my arm a pinch to make sure that I wasn't dreaming. I winced from the pain. *Nope, I'm not dreaming. That was real.*

"I love you," he said to me. "I mean that. I really do."

It took me a second to come out of my stunned stupor. I gave him another quick peck on the lips and whispered, "I love you too."

He turned around to face the opposite direction, and I put my arm around him. His hand met mine, and we laid that way until morning.

What did this mean for our relationship? I hope this wouldn't feel weird the next day. I was more content than I'd been in a long time, but I also felt a sense of anxiety about what the future held for us.

I closed my eyes and said a small prayer. It was the first time in a while that I had prayed without being coaxed to do so. *Dear Lord, if you are out there, I pray that you can watch over us. And give me confirmation that this is the right thing to do.* I still felt conflicted and wasn't sure about the best way to put it into words.

Just look after us, please, and keep us safe and happy. This I pray in Jesus' precious name. Amen. It occurred to me I was copying my mom's manner of praying. Maybe I was more Baptist than I cared to admit.

I could hear Ricky's heavy breathing by now. He was sound asleep. I kept my arm around him, and I held him tight. Soon everything went dark.

ACKNOWLEDGEMENT

I, first and foremost, want to thank everyone who supported me during my very nerve-wracking coming out. I remember being scared to death the first time I told someone, but I have gotten so much love and support. Yes, I also received some backlash and lost friends over it, but the reactions were overwhelmingly positive.

I want to give a big shout-out to my editor, Liz, who did a great job in helping me get my manuscript to where it is. This story was very personal, and I feel she handled it with sensitivity and care.

Also, to my cover designer, Hedri, He created a masterpiece that really encompassed the feeling and mood of what I was trying to convey, and I am pleased that I was introduced to his work.

And last but not least, thank you very much to everyone who reads this. I really appreciate all of your continued support.

ABOUT THE AUTHOR

Steven Lundle

Steven is a filmmaker and writer who was born in Barrhead, Canada, and raised in the small hamlet of Rochfort Bridge. He started writing when still a kid and mainly focuses on horror and fantasy, but he was also influenced by his upbringing, particularly being gay while raised in a strict Christian home, and he likes to write about those experiences as well.

BOOKS BY THIS AUTHOR

The Doll: And Other Short Stories

A collection of short dark stories about childhood fears, loneliness, and loss.

- Olivia receives a doll, but something seems off
-Rocky is having issues with a strange kid at daycare.
-Timmy sees things as he comes to terms with the death of his grandmother.
-Amiya desperately tries to find her friends who have disappeared in Tokyo.
-And what's behind that door that keeps reappearing in a dream?

"The Doll: and other short stories" is a collection of stories that deal with the dark and the supernatural.

Printed in Great Britain
by Amazon